MURDERS GALORE

Murders Galore is a collection of six stories that range through time and place from a World War Two military post, to a Midwestern industrial city, to a boys' vacation camp, to a transcontinental streamliner. The macabre methods and motives involved are as varied as the venues, but the result in each case is — *murder*! Beginning with *The Square Root of Dead*, in which a doomed mathematics professor devises, in his final moments, an ingenius way to identify his killer . . .

Books by Richard A. Lupoff
in the Linford Mystery Library:

THE UNIVERSAL HOLMES
THE CASES OF CHASE AND
DELACROIX
ONE MURDER AT A TIME
THE EVIL BELOW
ROOKIE COP

RICHARD A. LUPOFF

MURDERS GALORE

Complete and Unabridged

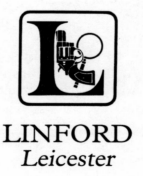

LINFORD
Leicester

First published in Great Britain

First Linford Edition
published 2015

A catalogue record for this book is available
from the British Library.

ISBN 978–1–4448–2592–3

Published by
F. A. Thorpe (Publishing)
Anstey, Leicestershire

Set by Words & Graphics Ltd.
Anstey, Leicestershire
Printed and bound in Great Britain by
T. J. International Ltd., Padstow, Cornwall

This book is printed on acid-free paper

Contents

THE SQUARE ROOT
OF DEAD

Professor Harker lay in the grotesque, unembarrassed posture of death, his arms sprawled out, his right leg doubled under him, his eyes staring up unblinkingly at the final unknown. He looked mildly surprised, as though this was not the answer he expected.

Lieutenant Loman stood to one side, his ungloved hands thrust under his arms for warmth, and looked at the body while his partner, Sergeant Stametti, and the lab men finished the methodical detail work that had to be completed before the corpse could be moved. They photographed it from all the necessary, undignified angles, dusted all the plausible surfaces for fingerprints — not likely out here in the middle of the snow-covered quadrangle — and conducted a painstaking search of the immediate area, bagging whatever they found, no matter how mundane or meaningless: cigarette butts, soda bottles, all the detritus with which the human race clutters up the surface of this planet.

Loman had ruled out anything clearly dropped before the snow started that evening, for which the lab crew was properly grateful. It was evident that, when Professor James Conrad Harker had met his rendezvous with that greater calculus in the sky, the snow had just about stopped falling.

A thin man joined Loman, carefully skirting the yellow rope the lab crew had put up to circle and define the death scene. 'You're Lieutenant Loman,' the thin man said, extending a gloved hand. 'I'm Professor Pyne. If there's any way in which I can help . . . I mean, I don't know what I could do but — this is startling, you know. I mean . . . '

'You knew Professor Harker?' Loman asked, looking into Pyne's slightly bulging eyes while he took the offered hand.

'We've been colleagues for over twenty years,' Professor Pyne said, shifting his gaze to stare down at the body. 'I'm head of the department now. Can't they cover

4

up the body? I mean . . . '

'What department, Professor?'

'What? Oh — mathematics. James Conrad Harker was one of the leading algebraic topologists in the country — in the world. Can you tell me what happened to him?'

'That's what we're trying to find out. He appears to have been stabbed, but we don't know as yet with what, by whom or why. Who told *you* about it, Professor, and why did you come down here?'

Pyne bristled. 'You don't think — '

'It's my job, Professor,' Loman interrupted, 'asking questions. I very seldom know the answers in advance or I wouldn't bother asking the question.'

'A student — one of Harker's graduate students, actually — called me up and told me about it. I came down because I felt I should. As head of the department, I mean, and his friend. To see if there was anything I could do.'

Loman nodded. 'Tell me about Professor Harker,' he said. 'What sort of man was he?'

'Brilliant,' Pyne said. 'Can we — ah

— talk somewhere else?'

'In a minute, Professor.' The ambulance had just arrived, and Sergeant Stametti looked over to Loman with a mute question. Loman nodded, and the body was carefully picked up and placed on the stretcher. Now the area under the body would be examined, and Harker's clothing would be cursorily searched, pending the complete examination at the morgue.

'It's Professor Harker's personality I'm interested in,' Loman said, leading Pyne away from the scene. 'Was he gregarious and friendly, or surly and private? Did he have a temper? Was he the sort of nit-picking pedant who provokes fits of temper in others?'

They walked together toward Euclid Avenue, which bordered the near side of the quadrangle, while Professor Pyne thought that over. It was just after eleven at night, and most of the shops were closed. Two coffee houses were still open, and Loman and Pyne headed into the nearer.

'Professor Harker was a friendly,

easygoing man,' Pyne said. 'He had a variety of interests outside his field, like glass collecting, *Go*, science fiction and heuristic programming techniques.'

'*Go*?' Loman asked. 'Isn't that a game?'

'Right, Lieutenant. Something like chess, only not.'

'And what's this 'heuristic programming'? You mean, computers?'

'That's right. A heuristic program is one which, so to speak, allows the computer to learn from experience. Not to make the same mistake twice, I mean.'

'I didn't know they could do that,' Loman said. 'I thought all a computer could do was add and subtract, only incredibly fast.'

'That's basically right,' Professor Pyne agreed. 'That's what makes heuristic programming such a challenge. It's like teaching an adding machine to think.'

Sergeant Stametti pushed through the door of the coffee shop and hurried over to Loman's table, his feet distributing snow over the hardwood floor as he stamped down the aisle. 'Something for you, Lieutenant,' he said, setting a small plastic box gently on the table. 'Found it under the body. It's one of them hand computers.'

'Calculators,' Professor Pyne corrected absently, staring with interest at the little mechanism. 'It's his — Professor Harker's, I mean. We gave it to him as sort of a joke for his last birthday. He was fifty-five.'

'It's lit up,' Loman said, looking at the bright, ruby-red number 3, which shone up at him.

'That's why I brought it in to you,' Stametti explained. 'I doubt if even a math professor would walk about carrying the number three all lit up. I thought it might be a last message, or something.'

'A dying message, eh? Why not? I've been on the Homicide Detail for eight years — I deserve a dying message. Tell me, Professor Pyne, does the number three mean anything to you?'

Pyne smiled. 'I could probably give you a two-hour lecture on the number three,' he said. 'But if you mean in specific relation to Professor Harker, no.'

8

'Nothing at *all*, Professor? He wasn't a member of a three-man committee, or holding a three-student class, or maybe on some list where the members are always put in the same order? You know: one, two, three — '

'Not anything meaningful,' Pyne said. 'Not that I can think of — I mean. Harker does — did — have three graduate student research assistants in this office.'

'Were they listed in any order?'

'If so, it would be alphabetical. Let's see: it's Mr. Bliss, Miss Bohle, and Mr. Quipper. And, of course, there's the faculty list for the department. But I believe Harker himself is number three. *Was.*'

'*Great!*' Lieutenant Loman said.

Pyne stared down at the calculator. 'Wait a second!' he said. 'It might be . . . may I?' He reached for the machine.

Loman pushed it over and watched Professor Pyne as he carefully pushed down the button-switch in the lower right-hand corner marked (−). As he did, a whole row of numbers lit up in front of the 3.

'It's as I remembered,' Pyne said. 'The

9

device automatically suppresses all but the last digit after thirty seconds.'

'What for, Professor?' Sergeant Stametti asked, staring curiously at the plastic box.

'To save the battery,' Pyne explained. 'The thing that draws most of the current in these devices is the lighting display, so many of them are made to suppress the display after thirty seconds except for the last digit to remind you that you're holding a number.'

Lieutenant Loman pulled absently at the corners of his trim moustache and examined the number now glowing up at him. It was 2 1 9 8. 2 1 1 3.

'Could this be part of some problem that Professor Harker was working on?' he asked.

'I wouldn't think so,' Pyne said. 'Topologists don't work with numbers, actually.'

'Then why did you get him the calculator?' Loman asked.

'It was sort of a joke,' Pyne said. 'Professor Harker had an absolute eidetic memory for numbers. He never had to write down addresses or phone numbers. Each number had a separate personality for him. I mean, that's the way he described it. But he absolutely couldn't add or subtract. We got him the calculator to balance his checkbook.'

'Phone number, eh?' Loman said. 'Maybe . . . no, it's too long.'

'Say,' Stametti said, 'maybe it spelled out something, like the name of the guy who attacked him. We didn't find a pen or a pencil on him. Maybe this was the professor's only way to name his killer.'

'Right,' Loman agreed. 'Now all we have to do is go up to old two-one-nine-eight and tell him the game's up.'

'No, Lieutenant, really. My kid showed me. You can turn the thing upside down and get words. Here, I'll show you.'

'Wait a second,' Loman said. He copied the number off the display into his notebook, and then handed the calculator to Stametti.

'Here, look,' Stametti said. He cleared the instrument and tapped in 3-2-0-0-8. '*There!*' He handed the calculator back to Lieutenant Loman.

'So?' Loman asked. He frowned.

'Turn it upside down,' Stametti instructed.

'Read the dial upside down.'

Loman obeyed instructions and read B-O-O-Z-E in the amber lights. '*Well!*' he said. 'Clever. The eight is a 'B' and so forth. Let's see what it says with Professor Harker's number.' He reentered the number that had been on the machine and then turned it upside down and stared at the result. 'It doesn't mean anything to me,' he said finally. 'And I really thought we had something for a minute. What do you think, Professor Pyne?'

Pyne examined the upside down display. 'E-I-I-Z-point-B — could be an R maybe — I-Z. No, I can't say it means anything to me. Sorry. Frankly, I doubt if it would have occurred to Professor Harker to play that sort of game with his calculator. I mean, he didn't think that way.'

Loman stood up and stuck the little calculator in his pocket. 'Thanks for your help, Professor,' he said. 'Would you please give the full names and addresses of Professor Harker's three research assistants to Sergeant Stametti so he can question them in the morning? I'm going home to bed now so I can dream about numbers.'

★ ★ ★

Lieutenant Loman didn't see Stametti again until eleven the next morning, when the sergeant slammed into the office in his usual enthusiastic way. 'Busy morning,' Stametti said. 'Got a lot for you. Don't know what good it is, any of it. What're you doing?'

'I borrowed an instruction manual from the store that sells these calculators,' Loman said. 'I figure that if I know how to work it right, I'll have a better chance of figuring out what in hell Harker was trying to tell us.'

'I been thinking about that, Lieutenant,' Stametti said. He paused.

'And?' Loman prompted as Stametti stared morosely down at the instruction book in his hand.

'It don't mean anything, Lieutenant. You'd better give it up and just read my reports when I get them typed up.'

Loman and Stametti had a long-established system of working together — Stametti dug up the information and Loman and analyzed and interpreted it.

Each was particularly good at what he did, and each admired the other for his particular ability. They worked well together.

Lieutenant Loman put the booklet down and leaned back in his wooden swivel chair. 'Let's hear it, Stametti — why should I give it up?'

'I've been questioning the three grad students and assembling information on their backgrounds,' Stametti said, 'and it's odds on that one of them did it. All three of them have possible motives, and as far as I can tell they're the only ones. Harker didn't have any money, he didn't have a job anyone else wanted, his wife died three years ago and he hasn't been seeing anyone since, and everyone at the university respected him.'

'Good work,' Loman said. 'Get it typed up and I'll stare at it. Why does that mean that the number on the calculator isn't a dying message? The professor didn't have anything to write with on him when he died.'

'He wouldn't be obscure,' Stametti said. 'He'd have no reason to leave a number with four places on each side of the decimal point. No reason at all.'

'Explain.'

'Sure. The three research assistants are named Robert Quipper, Jan Bliss, and Susan Bohle.' Stametti paused expectantly, staring at Loman.

'Go on,' Loman said, a trace of annoyance showing in his voice.

'Sure. I thought you'd see it. You can write all three names upside down, like I showed you, on the calculator. Here. Look.' Stametti picked the calculator up from Loman's desk and tapped 808 into it. Upside down it became BOB. Then he demonstrated how 55178 became BLISS and 37408 reverse to BOHLE.

'I see,' Loman said thoughtfully. 'So if Harker could name his attacker that easily — '

'Right,' Stametti agreed. 'He had no reason to leave two-one-nine-eight-point-two-one-one-three as a clue if he could leave an easily understandable eight-o-eight.'

'Perhaps Mister eight-o-eight isn't the killer,' Loman suggested. 'Or Bliss or

Bohle either. Perhaps it's more complex than that. Or even if you're right about no one else having a reason to eliminate Harker, maybe it was a nut killer.'

'If it was a nut killer,' Sergeant Stametti said, 'then that number is a nut clue, and you'll never figure what it means.' He put the calculator back down on the desk.

Loman shook his head in disgust. 'You're probably right,' he said. 'Go type up those reports and get them to me, so I can get the feel of these three students.'

Sergeant Stametti went off to his own desk, leaving Loman staring down at the calculator. He punched BOB and squared it. Then he took the square root of BLISS and the reciprocal of BOHLE, and no matter how long he stared at the results they were merely numbers, nothing more.

About an hour later, slightly after noon, Stametti returned to Loman's desk and flopped a set of typed forms on the battered wood surface in front of the Lieutenant.

'Thanks, Stametti,' Loman said. 'I'll look at them after lunch. I'm trying to make up the duty roster for the next month.'

'How'd you get stuck with *that* job?' Stametti asked him. 'You'd better look over the reports now.'

'It's the Captain's new policy,' Loman said. 'He believes, all of a sudden, in delegating authority. Why had I better look over the reports now?'

'Because they're all going to be here at one-thirty to talk to you. I thought I told you.'

Loman stiff-armed the worksheet to the back of the desk with his right palm. 'No, Sergeant,' he said, 'you didn't mention that.'

'I arranged it,' Stametti said. 'We don't want this case to drag on, so I figured you'd wrap it up this afternoon after you read my reports.'

Loman stared at Stametti, but could make nothing out of his bland expression. 'Well then,' Loman said, 'I guess I'd better get at those reports. All three graduate students are coming at one-thirty?'

'Right. And the professor, too.'

'Professor Pyne?'

'Right. *Him*.'

'Why?'

'He's a possible. Not a probable, but a possible.'

'What's *his* motive?'

'Try professional jealousy. Harker was more highly regarded as a mathematician. I have it from the rest of the department. Pyne's been jealous of Harker for twenty years. A thing like that can build up. It sounds like a slim motive for murder, but people have been killed for a lot less. Pyne might be slightly batty on the subject.'

'Any sign of that?'

'No. Apparently they were good friends. Anything else you want, let me know.'

'Ham and swiss on rye toast, light coffee, no sugar — and don't forget the pickle.'

'You eating lunch at your desk? I thought we'd go to Pronzini's and have a steak.'

'You're the one made the one-thirty appointment. Now let me read these reports and see if I get any bright ideas.'

'Right. One ham and swiss on rye.' Stametti gave a gesture vaguely reminiscent of a salute and left.

On top of Stametti's stack of papers was the Medical Examiner's preliminary report. The ME confirmed what had been apparent last night. Professor Harker had been killed by a single thrust from a narrow, sharp instrument, which penetrated between the third and fourth ribs, severing the thoracic and carotid arteries, and causing almost immediate death by cutting off the blood supply to the brain. The professor was conscious for no more than a minute or two.

Just long enough, Loman thought, *to tap out that dying message on his calculator before he fell over. And I have to be smart enough to figure out what he meant. And he was a genius.*

Lieutenant Loman put the Medical Examiner's report aside. Below it were Stametti's reports on the four suspects, based on questioning each of them, and other, unverified data gathered that morning in the university's Math Department. He put the four reports side by side on the desk and read them alternately, line by line.

The vital statistics first: name, address, age, sex, phone number, occupation, police record (none admitted to having any — that was being checked), physical description. Then came the statements, which were put into narrative form in the style Loman called 'third person police impersonal'.

NAME Quipper, Robert L.
AGE 26 SEX M
ADDRESS 3132 Percy Street
PHONE 483-2132

Robert Quipper, the oldest of the three graduate students, had been a sergeant in the army, serving in Southeast Asia, before getting out and letting the government put him through school. He was in the midst of writing his doctoral thesis, and expected to have his degree by the end of the year.

It was known that he felt Professor Harker had walked off with an original idea of his and developed it without giving Quipper sufficient credit. The consensus in the Math Department was that what Harker had done was proper, and that the mention of Quipper in Harker's published paper was sufficient. But Quipper had a quick temper and had previously had several loud arguments with Harker on the subject.

NAME Bliss, Jan (nmi)
AGE 21 SEX M
ADDRESS 661½ Yeath Drive
PHONE 484-8947

Jan Bliss had never known any life except the world of science. A shy, introverted boy, he had turned to the study of the logical, invariable laws of the universe when he found himself unable to understand the whimsical, inconsistent customs of humanity. Normally Jan was quiet to the point of invisibility, although distantly polite if approached. The other students' opinions were that he would like to make friends if he knew how.

On very rare occasions, for no outward reason that anyone could tell, Jan fell into what psychologists call a fugue state, and would walk around as if in a dream, or perhaps visiting some other plane of existence. During these periods he tended to be destructive; at one party he methodically destroyed every salad plate in the house, leaving dinner plates, soup plates, cups, and glasses untouched.

He was never known to have harmed anyone or even attempted to while in this state. He was seeing a psychiatrist once every two weeks, all he could afford. The psychiatrist would not discuss his patient, but would say that he considered it extremely unlikely Jan could have stuck a knife into Professor James Conrad Harker.

NAME Bohle, Susan S.
AGE 23 SEX F
Address Rm D-12, 181 Tetra Street
PHONE 480-4896

Susan Bohle was an intelligent, articulate 23-year-old from a well-to-do family, who didn't encourage her choice of careers. Women were supposed to settle down and have children, according to Susan's mother. That being so, Susan's father felt graduate school was surely a waste of money. College, of course — everybody went to college. But why fool around getting a higher degree when you should be out getting a husband?

It was known that Professor Harker espoused similar views. Women belonged in the home, not the graduate school. Certainly no woman could ever hope to be a really top-flight mathematician. Competent, yes, but not genius. As a result of this prejudice, Harker was much harder on women students than on men. He was known to resent the pressure that had been brought to bear to make him take Susan Bohle as a research assistant. Common gossip had it that he was going to ease Susan out as quickly and as gracefully as possible with a Master's degree that, in this university, meant you weren't quite good enough to make your PhD.

Susan, who was really a brilliant student with an original intellect, was also very stubborn and tough-minded. She would have to be to buck her parents and her major professor. Was she tough-minded enough to stick a knife in Harker?

Stametti delivered the sandwich, and Lieutenant Loman paused long enough to eat half before turning the reports over and reading the suspects' statements as to where they had been when Professor Harker was murdered.

None of them had what you'd call an alibi. Robert Quipper had been home brushing up for the calculus course. He was a teaching assistant, half-expecting Professor Harker to call and make arrangements to talk over a paper they were preparing. The professor had never called.

Jan Bliss had been out at a meeting of the Society of the Round Table, a group dedicated to bringing back the social graces and customs of the early Middle Ages. They dressed in period costumes, and Jan seemed more at home in the garb of an earlier time.

Twenty-five people were ready to swear he attended, but the hall they met in was only a few blocks from the part where Harker was killed. He could have slipped out long enough to make the round trip before he was missed. And he had been

24

wearing a three-foot sword.

Susan Bohle claimed that she was visiting a boyfriend for the night. But, in a curious reversal of traditional morality, she refused to give his name, saying he wouldn't want to get involved. It was Susan who had called Professor Pyne, having herself been called by a friend and told of Harker's death.

So the identity of her boyfriend must be common knowledge on campus if someone had known to call her there. It could be obtained, if necessary. Of course, there was the possibility that she knew of the killing because she had participated in it, and no one had called her at all. In which case there was probably no boyfriend.

Professor Pyne, Stametti's fourth suspect, was at home all evening until he received the phone call from Susan Bohle. His wife would swear to that. But the testimony of wives in regard to their husbands was always suspect.

Lieutenant Loman stacked the reports together and weighed them in both hands. One of these four? Which one? If only the professor had been carrying a portable typewriter with him instead of a calculator. He could have just tapped out the name.

The name? Loman turned the reports over and stared at the headings, with the typed-in names and addresses. *Perhaps he did*, Loman thought. *Perhaps that's just what the professor did*.

A half hour later Stametti came into the office to find Loman leaning back in his chair, folding a paper airplane. Several others were distributed about the office.

'They're here,' Stametti said, ignoring the aerodynamic experiment. 'Which one do you want to see fist?'

'I'll see them all,' Loman told him. 'Come on!'

'You've *got it!*' Stametti said, doing his best to keep up with Loman's long strides without breaking into a trot. 'I can tell. You've pegged the killer.'

'I have,' Loman admitted, doing his best not to sound smug.

'Are you sure?'

'Sure enough to have obtained a warrant. The killer's rooms are being searched even as we stand here waiting for the elevator.'

'Something I gave you?' Stametti demanded.

'Right — something you gave me. And something Professor Harker gave us.'

'The number on the calculator?'

'Right.'

'Then it means something?'

'It does — and it doesn't. Come along. The elevator's stalled again.'

They went down the wide stairs in the old precinct building in the second floor, then down a long corridor, past the Juvenile Division, past Safe and Loft, to the large interrogation room Stametti had left the suspects in. 'What do you mean, 'It does — and it doesn't'?' Stametti asked.

'We were looking at it wrong.'

'Upside down?'

'No, backward. You'll see.'

They entered a room. The four suspects were sitting around the conference table with a litter of plastic cups of coffee and cigarette butt-filled ashtrays in front of them.

Lieutenant Loman looked them over, sorting them out in his mind. Professor Pyne was farthest away, facing the door. The girl was, of course, Susan Bohle. She was very pretty, with long blonde hair and piercing hazel eyes. Somehow Loman hadn't thought she'd be pretty. The slender young man with the aquiline nose who kept his left hand in front of his mouth, must be Jan Bliss. The stocky man with the aggressive chin who kept his chair teetering precariously back would then be Robert Quipper.

'Good afternoon,' Loman said. 'I'm Lieutenant Loman. And you are,' — he named them, left to right — 'Mr. Bliss, Miss Bohle, Professor Pyne, Mr. Quipper.'

Three of them nodded. Quipper straightened his chair with a crash and leaned forward across the table. 'Look here,' he said. 'What's all this about? Why are we here?'

'I apologize for the inconvenience,' Loman said. 'At least to three of you, I apologize. You see, some new information has come to light.'

'New — ah — information?' Professor

Pyne asked, frowning.

'Yes.' Loman turned to Robert Quipper. 'You told my investigator last night and waited for Professor Harker to call.'

'That's right,' Quipper said.

'The telephone company records show that you received that call,' Loman said. He nodded to Stametti, who circled around to stand behind Quipper's chair.

'That's ridiculous,' Quipper said, trying to keep an eye on Stametti and stare belligerently at Loman.

'How is it ridiculous?' Loman asked. 'Because he called you from a pay phone? But there is a record of the call, and which pay phone it was from. It was the last call from that phone, and Professor Harker's prints are all over the handset.'

'You have the right to remain silent,' Stametti intoned, reading from the little card in his hand.

Quipper listened impassively as his rights were read to him. 'I'm not saying anything,' he said, when Stametti put the card back in his pocket.

'That's your right,' Loman told him.

Quipper shook his head. 'The god

damn phone,' he said.

'We have more,' Loman said. 'We have a witness that places you at the scene of the crime — that names you directly. I'm telling you this with the others present so you won't think I'm playing some kind of cat-and-mouse game and taking each of you aside to accuse you of the murder. You killed James Harker, Mr. Quipper, and I know it.'

'What witness?' Professor Pyne asked. 'Who?'

'Not 'who', Professor,' Loman said, pulling the little calculator from his pocket. 'This is my witness. Professor Harker did name his killer, and it was Robert Quipper he named.'

'How?' Pyne asked.

'Why didn't he just write 808?' Stametti asked.

'As Professor Pyne told us last night,' Loman said, 'Professor Harker didn't play games like that. Let's look at what he did. We found this number in the machine — 2 1 9 8. 2 1 1 3.

'Now there are three possibilities. One, that the number was there by some sort of cosmic accident, having nothing to do with the professor or his murder. I rejected that on the grounds that the professor wouldn't have left the calculator turned on as if he wasn't using it. The battery would have died in a few hours. As a matter of fact, the full charge on the battery when we found the device shows that it wasn't turned on much before Professor Harker's death.

'Two, that Professor Harker put the number 2198.2113 in the calculator as a dying message, hoping it would tell us who killed him.'

Professor Pyne leaned forward. 'And you say it did? That number somehow implicates Quipper as Professor Harker's assassin?' He pulled out a pen and a notebook, wrote the number down, and stared at it.

A uniformed officer came in behind Lieutenant Loman and handed him a note. He read it, and then put it in his pocket and went on. 'Not directly,' he said. 'For that we get to the third possibility — that Professor Harker actually put some other number down in the calculator, but that the number was somehow altered before we saw it.

'For example, as the professor fell he might have inadvertently pressed one of the buttons, or it might have knocked against the pavement. A button that would alter the number that the calculator was holding. Say, the square button, or the square root button.

'Let's test that out. Now, if we square the number we're working with, we get' — he pressed the x^2 button on the calculator and read out, '4 8 3 2 1 3 2 . 9.'

'Which brings nothing immediately to mind as the identity of the murderer. If we, on the other hand, press the square root function' — and Lieutenant Loman put the original number back in the machine and pushed the button marked $\sqrt{x}$, getting 4 6 . 8 8 5 0 8 6.'

Professor Pyne stared at the number, trying to read its mystical significance. 'So?'

'So we were doing it backward. The professor *did* punch a number into his calculator. Then as he fell he hit the square root button.

'The number he punched in was Robert Quipper's phone number — 4 8 3 2 1 3 3.'

'But the number you get when you square our number is 4832132.9,' Sergeant Stametti objected. 'I admit it's uncomfortably close, but why the difference? How did the 3 change to a 2.9?'

'Try it,' Loman invited, handing Stametti the calculator. 'Put in the phone number first, then hit the square root button.'

Sergeant Stametti did as instructed. He tapped Quipper's phone number into the machine, then took the square root. He stared down at the familiar number they had found on the machine.

'But when we reverse it,' Loman said, leaning over the table and hitting the square button, 'it ends in 2.9.'

'Of course!' Professor Pyne said. 'The calculator rounds off the last figure on numbers that exceed capacity. This causes the error when the process is reversed.'

'And we didn't look for a phone number,' Lieutenant Loman said, 'because the results had eight digits. But we were doing it backwards.'

'It'll never stand up in court,' Quipper said.

Loman took the note he had just received and flipped it in front of Quipper. 'We got a warrant,' he said, 'and searched your apartment. Found an old hunting knife in a leather sheath. If that fresh stain on the blade is human blood, you're in trouble. Along with what we got from the phone company I think we'll be able to put you away.'

'You don't understand,' Quipper said.

'I never do,' Lieutenant Loman said. 'Sergeant, take this gentleman downstairs.'

BENNING'S SCHOOL
FOR BOYS

Private Nicholas Train was sitting on his bunk polishing his combat boots, wondering if he hadn't made a mistake when he passed up the chance for an exemption. They considered cops essential, the Selective Service Board did, and he could have filed papers and stayed out of the draft, stayed safely at home. Pounding a beat in Brooklyn wasn't exactly cherry duty, but it beat the hell out of getting shot at by the krauts or the nips and maybe coming home with some pieces missing, or maybe in a box.

But, what the hell, he hadn't liked Hitler from the start, and when his Chinese girlfriend asked him to take her to Mott Street for roast duck lo mein and he'd got an earful from her about what was going on in China, he decided that the nips were no better than the Nazis.

Pearl Harbor was the last straw. He was ready to sign up the next morning but there would have been nobody to take care of his mother so he kept pounding his beat, mooning around the house when he was off duty, and taking his Chinese girlfriend to Mott Street whenever she asked him to.

Then, almost a year after Pearl Harbor, Mom died. The day after the funeral Train had dressed in civvies, put in his papers at the precinct and signed up for the United States Army.

And here he was halfway through Basic, sitting on his bed polishing his boots. Somebody had brought a portable radio into the barracks and they were playing Christmas music. A couple of guys were writing letters home. There was a lazy poker game going on, the cards smacking down and coins rattling on a foot-locker. And Private Aaron Hirsch was sitting on his bunk crying.

'What's the matter with you, Jewboy?' That was Private Joseph Francis Xavier Schulte, former altar boy, former star full-back of St. Aloysius's Academy, designated barracks anti-Semite. 'You got no right to cry at Christmas carols, you Christ-killer.'

38

Hirsch jumped up. His face turned the same color as his crinkled red hair. 'Shut the hell up, Saint. What I do is my business.'

'Oh, listen to the little kike. Ain't you tough, Hirsch? You want some of what I gave that Jewboy halfback from Maimonides? I put that bastard in the hospital, in case you don't remember.'

'*Cut it out!*'

Ah, the voice of authority. The soldier standing in the doorway wore two chevrons on his winter ODs. His olive drab uniform was neatly pressed. In it he looked like a military fashion plate compared to the trainees in their baggy fatigues. He wore a brassard around one sleeve, designating him as the corporal of the guard.

'Hey, Pops!' He pointed a finger at Train. 'Grab your piece and report to the company office. Captain Coughlin wants to see you.'

'Me?'

'Yeah, you.'

'Captain Coffin?'

'Very funny. Don't let him hear you call him that.'

'What's he want me for?' This had to be something serious. If it wasn't, Corporal Bowden would have handled it himself, or at most Sergeant Dillard. The company first sergeant was as close to God as they ever saw, most days. Officers were some kind of exotic creatures who kept to themselves and spoke to the GIs only through sergeants and corporals.

'Christ, Pops, how the hell do I know?' Bowden took a few steps and clicked the portable radio into silence. 'Hey, it's Saturday morning. You guys get a few hours off to polish your gear and get your letters written. What's this?'

He picked up the playing cards and the cash that was laid out on a foot-locker between two cots. 'You guys know there's no gambling allowed in the barracks. And it's payday. How do you have any mazuma left to play for? Now I have to confiscate this evidence.' He stuffed the cards in one pocket and the money in another. 'I don't know, I don't know, how are we ever going to make soldiers out of you sad sacks?'

Nick Train had shoved his feet into his

boots and tucked his fatigue jacket into his trousers. 'Coughlin really wants to see me, Bowden?'

'No, I'm just trying to ruin your Saturday. Of course he wants to see you.'

'No idea why?'

'Nope.'

Train smoothed out the blankets on his bunk, took his Garrand rifle down from the rack near the barracks door and headed out into the wintry Georgia air. For a December morning the day wasn't too cold, certainly no colder than Train was used to in Brooklyn. The sky was clear and sparkling and the sun was a brilliant disk. There were a few patches of snow still on the ground. The last snowfall had been three days ago. Train held his rifle at port arms and quick-timed across the company area toward the office.

The building behind him was new construction, whitewashed wooden walls under a green tar-paper roof. It would probably be hot as blazes in the summer but he wouldn't know that. It was definitely freezing cold in the winter.

First Sergeant Dillard was working at his desk in the company office. He looked up when Train arrived, then back at his paperwork. He didn't say anything, didn't indicate why Train had been summoned.

Train stood at attention facing the First Sergeant's desk.

After a while, Dillard looked up again and grunted. 'Go back to the door and knock the snow off your boots. What kind of pigsty do you think this is?'

Train complied. Then he returned to stand in front of Dillard, his Garrand at his side, butt on the linoleum floor beside his polished boot.

'Captain Coughlin wants to see you, Train.'

'Corporal Bowden told me. What's it's about, Sarge?'

'Sergeant.'

'Sorry. Sergeant.'

'I don't know.' First Sergeant Martin Dillard shook his head. 'I don't know, but it's something big. He's got Lieutenant McWilliams in there with him. And I heard some walloping a while ago.' He shook his head again. 'Just go knock on the door, Train, and maybe say a prayer while you're at it.'

Lieutenant Phillips McWilliams opened the door to the Captain's office when Train knocked. McWilliams was gussied up in officer's dark greens, the silver bars shining on his shoulder straps like miniature neon bulbs, the US insignia and crossed rifles of the infantry on his lapels polished to a sheen. He even affected the Sam Browne belt that every other officer Train knew had abandoned.

Train almost expected him to be wearing a parade ground saber with his uniform, but he wasn't. Instead, there was a holster hooked to his uniform belt, the regulation holster issued to officers along with their .45 caliber Colt automatics.

The lieutenant jerked his head toward Captain Samuel Coughlin's desk.

Train crossed the room, halted, thumped his rifle butt on the floor and executed a sharp rifle salute, the way he'd been taught a few weeks ago.

Captain Coughlin bounced his forefinger off his right eyebrow, then folded his hands in front of him on his desk. Even in

December he sat in his shirtsleeves, his uniform jacket with the railroad tracks on the shoulders on a nearby hanger. Train had never been in the Captain's office before. He kept his posture but even so he was able to see the pictures on the freshly whitewashed wall behind the captain. There was a standard shot of President Roosevelt, one of old General Pershing and one of General Marshall, and a blow-up that must have been made in France during the First War. It showed a very young Samuel Coughlin standing rigidly while an officer who had to be Douglas MacArthur himself pinned a medal on his khaki tunic.

There was a fire axe on Captain Coughlin's desk. Behind him, Train saw another doorway. The door-frame and the door had been damaged, Train guessed, by the fire-axe.

'They call you Pops, don't they?' Captain Coughlin asked.

Train said, 'Yes, sir.'

'Why is that?'

'They're mostly kids, sir. All of them, in fact. Seventeen, eighteen, nineteen years old. I guess Hirsch is a little older, maybe twenty. They think I'm an old man.'

'How old are you, Train?'

'I'm twenty-four, sir.'

'Used to be a police officer, did you?'

Captain Coughlin knew damned well that Train used to be a police officer. He knew how old he was, knew everything else that was in Train's 201 file, the personnel folder that every man Jack in the Army had. Still, he answered.

'Yes, sir.'

'Twenty-four.' The Captain smiled sadly. 'Twenty-four and they call you Pops. Well, I guess we did the same thing in '18.' The Captain's face was leathery and etched with lines, his hair graying at the temples.

Captain Coughlin jerked his thumb in the direction of the damaged doorway. 'Do you know what's in there, Train?'

'No, sir.'

'It's the company safe room. We keep classified information locked up in there. What passes for classified information in this kindergarten. We also put the payroll in there the night before payday.'

Captain Coughlin pushed himself back from his desk and stood up. He moved toward the damaged doorway. 'Take a look, soldier. Go ahead in there.'

It was only a few steps. Once inside the safe room Train stopped. The safe door hung open. Train couldn't tell what if anything was inside. A coffee mug stood on top of the safe. Corporal Miller, the company pay clerk, sat beside it in a battered wicker chair. His arms hung over the arms of the chair, almost but not quite dragging on the linoleum. His head was canted to one side. His hair was matted with blood. He wasn't moving, and Train had seen enough bodies in the line of duty as a cop to know that he was dead.

Even so, he flashed an inquiry to the Captain, got a suggestion of a nod in return, then felt the side of Miller's neck, searching for a pulse. There was no pulse. The body was cold. There were no windows in the room. Most of the light came from a shaded fixture hanging by a long cord from the ceiling, casting macabre shadows on Miller's face. A little more light filtered through the open doorway from the Captain's office.

Train turned around. Captain Coughlin was standing with his fists balled and balanced on his hips. 'Poor fellow,' Coughlin murmured. 'He was one of our good boys, you know. Religious as all get-out. Chapel every Sunday. Rosary in his pocket, Missal in his foot-locker. Poor bastard.'

Coughlin didn't use strong language very often.

Lieutenant McWilliams stood in the doorway, looking like a photographer's model.

Turning back to Corporal Miller, Train observed that Miller, too, had been issued a .45. The holster hung from Miller's belt, the butt of the automatic visible from where Train stood.

'I should probably call the Provost Marshal right now,' Captain Coughlin announced. 'It's his business eventually, in any case. But they're looking to put me out to pasture. I shouldn't tell you this, Train, I wouldn't tell it to any of the kids in this outfit, but I'm going to rely on your maturity. If I turn up with a dead payroll clerk and an empty safe, they'll decide I can't cut it any more and I'm out of here on a pension. Not for me, Sunny Jim! Not with a big war going on.'

He walked around the safe and the wicker chair with its motionless occupant. 'No, sir, not for Samuel Coughlin, USA. If we can solve this thing and present a solution to the Provost Marshal instead of a mystery, I just might get out of this kindergarten and get a chance to do some fighting before I'm through.'

'I don't know if that's wise, Captain.'

Lieutenant McWilliams had a cultured voice. He was the opposite of the Captain.

Train knew — everybody in the unit knew — that Coughlin was a mustang. He'd been an enlisted man in the First World War, earned a commission and spent the Roaring Twenties and the Depression years soldiering at backwoods Army posts. Now he was overage in grade and hanging on by his fingernails.

But McWilliams was the scion of a high society family. Barracks rumors claimed that his mother had wanted him to live out her own thwarted ambitions, to become a great and famous botanist. Either that, or enter the priesthood. Or both, like old Gregor Mendel. Instead, Old Man McWilliams was delighted when Junior opted for the United States Military Academy. All it took was a couple of phone calls and a generous campaign contribution to a United States senator, and young McWilliams was in. And he'd done his daddy proud. Cadet Captain, top ten per cent in his class, starting quarterback on the Army football team until a knee injury sidelined him for his senior season. And that might have been a blessing in disguise. The team had played badly and wound up the season losing the Army-Navy game for the third year in a row. At least Phillips McWilliams wouldn't be tarred with that loss. And the 1942 football season hadn't been much better, ending with another loss to Navy, a disgraceful fourteen-nothing shellacking.

But now Phillips McWilliams was a First Lieutenant in the United States

Army, executive officer of a training company at the Infantry School with a glittering future before him and only a careworn middle-aged Captain to climb over — at least for the moment. As an officer his duties weren't too rigorous. Train knew that. The ordinary GI's knew more about the lives of officers than the other way around. The people on the bottom always knew more about the people on top. That was one of life's constants. The trainees knew that Lieutenant McWilliams drove a shiny new Packard convertible, one of the last to roll off the line before the factory switched to war production, and he used it to cruise down broad Lumpkin Boulevard to Columbus or across the Chattahoochie River into Phenix City, Alabama, for a night of drinking and gambling and whoring pretty much whenever he felt like it.

McWilliams's Packard was just one car that all the trainees recognized. All the officers and NCOs in the permanent party had cars: Captain Coughlin's gray Plymouth, Sergeant Dillard's battered

Ford station wagon, Corporal Miller's little green Nash. They all bore Fort Benning tags, blue for the officers, red for the NCO's, all carefully logged in or out every time they passed through the post gatehouse.

Captain Coughlin was talking again. Train snapped back to the moment. To the — he grinned inwardly — crime scene. 'The First Sergeant called me this morning,' he said. 'Told me that he couldn't get a rise out of Miller. Corporal had spent the night in the safe room, same as every month the night before payday.'

The Captain paused. The room was silent. A platoon of officer candidates passed by outside. Train could hear their boots crashing on the frozen Georgia soil, hear them singing the unofficial Fort Benning Infantry School song.

High above the Chattahoochie/
Near the Upatois/
Stands our dear old alma mater/
Benning's School for Boys.

They were past the company office now, their voices growing fainter. But Train knew the song, as well.

Forward ever, backward never/
Follow me and die/
To the ports of embarkation/
Kiss your ass good-bye!

'Safe room door is secured with a hasp and padlock inside and out,' Captain Coughlin resumed. 'Not exactly Fort Knox, is it, but it's the best Uncle gives us to work with. Miller locked his side, I personally locked the outside. Sergeant Dillard, Lieutenant McWilliams and I all have keys to the outside lock, but that wouldn't get us in if Miller didn't open his. You see?'

Train grunted, then remembered himself and replied, 'Yes, sir.'

'That's why we had to use the fire-axe.' Lieutenant McWilliams sounded as if he disapproved of the whole proceeding.

Train knew the type. It was all beneath him. All beneath Mister Phillips Anderson McWilliams of the Newport and Palm

Beach McWilliamses.

Captain Coughlin grasped Train's bicep. The touch came as a shock. Officers didn't touch enlisted men. They might become contaminated.

Coughlin's grasp was remarkably powerful. His fingertips dug into Train's arm.

'What are you doing in this outfit anyway, Train?' He released Train's arm, stood eye-to-eye with him. Train was taller by four inches easily but he felt no advantage in facing this older man. 'Why are you here? Why didn't you apply for a commission? You ought to be in CID.'

'Criminal Investigation Division? Me, Captain?'

'I said that, didn't I?'

'Yes, sir. I — I just have to get through Basic first, don't I?'

'Course you do. All right. Look, I'm calling on your skills, soldier. You know how to deal with a crime scene. You know how to conduct an investigation.'

'Sir,' Lieutenant McWilliams interrupted. 'Sir, you're risking big trouble, sir. This is against regulations. Don't you want me to call the Provost Marshal? I really think that would be best, sir.'

Captain Coughlin said, 'Train, I want you to get to work on this. I'm relieving you of your other duties. You don't need the training anyway, you know everything a soldier needs to know.'

After another silence Coughlin asked, 'What do you need, Train?'

'I don't suppose you could get me an evidence kit, sir?'

'I'd have to get it from the Provost Marshal. The jig would be up.'

Train pursed his lips. He crossed the room, stood near one wall. He touched his fingers gingerly to the thin structure, then examined them. Fresh whitewash. He laid his rifle carefully on the floor, bolt lever upward. He went back to the doorway and examined the splintered wood.

'Who did this?' he asked.

'Sergeant Dillard.'

'Did you see him do it?'

'McWilliams and I were both witnesses.'

'What time was that?'

'McWilliams and I had breakfast

together at the mess hall. Sergeant Dillard came pounding in there to get us.' He looked at Lieutenant McWilliams.

The younger officer said, 'We ate at 0530 hours, Train. We were finishing our meal at approximately 0555 hours when Sergeant Dillard arrived. He was out of breath, seemed upset.'

Captain Coughlin grunted. 'Go on, McWilliams.'

The Lieutenant looked annoyed. For a moment Train was puzzled as to the reason, then he realized that Captain Coughlin had called him McWilliams, not Lieutenant McWilliams. Train held back a smile.

'We came through the day room, saw the lock was open from the outside. We tried to raise Miller but we couldn't. So the Captain had Sergeant Dillard use the fire axe.'

'And this room — ?' Train inquired.

'What about this room?'

'Did you touch anything? Move anything? Sir?'

McWilliams said, 'Nothing.'

Train stationed himself just inside the

doorway, studying the damaged wood and the area around it. The walls themselves were made of thin plasterboard. They had been recently whitewashed. Train bent closer to the door-jamb. He studied the wood and the adjacent plasterboard. He didn't say anything.

Behind him, Lieutenant McWilliams said, 'Aren't you even going to look at the corpse, Private?'

Train turned back, made what might have been an almost imperceptible bow to McWilliams, then addressed Captain Coughlin. 'I'd like to be alone at the crime scene, sir. If that's possible, please. I know, well, normally in police work there are a lot of professionals present. Photographers, fingerprint men, coroner's people, detectives. I'm not a detective myself, sir, but I've been at a lot of crime scenes and I was hoping for a promotion to detective. But we don't have those professionals here, so if I might, sir, I'd like to be alone in this room.'

'Not possible!' McWilliams sounded furious. 'This — this buck private, this plain GI — just because he used to be a flatfoot pounding a beat, wants to act like a big shot and order us around, Captain? Who does he think he is? He belongs back in his barracks, the Provost Marshal should be in charge.'

Captain Coughlin let out a sigh. 'Just go and — I tell you what, Lieutenant, scamper over to the mess hall and get us some coffee, will you?'

'I'll have Sergeant Dillard send a man.'

'No, McWilliams, you go yourself.'

This time Train couldn't restrain his grin. The Lieutenant looked as if Captain Coughlin had asked him to march around the parade ground in his skivvies. The air in the room was so full of tension you could have picked it up on a Zenith radio. But at last the Lieutenant took his leave.

Captain Coughlin said, 'Train, I'll be in my office. You call me if you need anything, otherwise just come on out when you finish in here.'

Captain Coughlin winked at Private Train. Yes, he did, he actually winked at the buck private. Then he left the safe room. He stopped and drew the damaged door shut behind him, the hole that the fire axe had gouged out admitting light from the outer room.

Train took one more, confirming look at the splintered wood and the adjacent plasterboard. The whitewash was recent enough to show traces of fingers dragging vertically on the door-jamb, then sliding horizontally onto the plasterboard.

Returning to the corpse, Train knelt and examined the two cold hands, first one and then the other. As he'd already noted, the fingertips were white. He lifted them and sniffed. There was whitewash on them.

He studied the wound on the side of Miller's head, feeling through the bloodied hair to try and determine whether the skull was damaged. It didn't seem to be. He scuttled across the linoleum and returned with his rifle. He stood over the body, holding the weapon so that its butt-plate was adjacent to the wound. He walked around the body and tried again, from behind.

It didn't fit. Miller had been hit with something smaller than a rifle butt.

Train studied the safe. He wasn't an

expert safe man, he didn't know very much about locks, but there was no evidence that the safe had been forced or blown open. If it had been, there would surely have been some reaction to the blast. Who had the combination of the safe? He'd have to find out.

In any case, Sergeant Dillard had tried to rouse Miller shortly before 0555 hours and failed to do so. He had a key to the outer lock and presumably used it — something else to check on — only to be stymied by the fact that the inner lock was dogged.

Captain Coughlin, Lieutenant McWilliams, and Sergeant Dillard all had keys to the outer lock. Only Miller had a key to the inner lock. Where was it? The lock itself was in Captain Coughlin's office, still attached to its hasp and the splintered wood that the hasp had been screwed to. But where was the key? Train searched Miller's pockets but failed to find it. The room was not brightly lighted, but Train searched anyway, going to his hands and knees and covering every square inch of floor.

The key turned up in the last place he looked — of course — a darkened corner of the room five or six feet away from the door.

Train stood up, squeezing the padlock key as if it could tell him what had happened. It couldn't, but he was convinced that the contents of the room could, if only he asked them the right questions.

Once again he studied the damage to Miller's head. He was convinced that was not the cause of death. Eventually the Provost Marshal's people or the Quartermaster's people would come and take away the body, and the Medics would perform an autopsy and pronounce cause of death, and Miller's parents would get a telegram from the Secretary of War and they would go out and buy a service flag with a gold star to hang in their window in place of the one with the blue star that Train was sure hung there now.

But he didn't want to wait.

He knelt in front of the corpse and studied its face. He leaned forward and smelled Miller's nostrils and his mouth but detected no odor. The features were relaxed in death. There was no rictus. He stood up and placed himself behind the wicker chair and tried to imagine Miller's last minutes.

Someone had struck Miller high on the skull on his left side. The blow didn't look serious enough to cause unconsciousness no less death. Who had struck Miller? Who could get into the safe room once it was locked from both inside and out? Only Captain Coughlin, Lieutenant McWilliams, or First Sergeant Dillard, and then only if Miller let them in by opening the inside lock.

He heard voices from the outer office and a moment later Captain Coughlin invited him to join him.

Lieutenant McWilliams was standing in front of Captain Coughlin's desk. There was a tray on the desk, with a steaming pot and three cups. First Sergeant Dillard stood nearby looking uncomfortable.

Captain Coughlin addressed Train. 'Come in, soldier. Pour yourself a cup of java.'

McWilliams, uniform pressed and buttons polished, was red-faced, his jaw clenched. With an obvious effort he said, 'Sir, I must protest. This soldier — there are only three cups — it's a violation of protocol — '

Coughlin waved his hand. 'We'll make do somehow, Lieutenant.'

McWilliams drew himself up, suddenly taller than he'd been. 'If the Captain will excuse me, sir, I have to return to my duties.'

Coughlin signaled Sergeant Dillard to approach. 'What's today's schedule, Sergeant?'

'We've been pushing the trainees pretty hard, sir. They have the morning off, then grenade drill this afternoon.'

'Good.'

'And, Captain — it's payday, sir. The men expect to be paid today.'

'All right.' Captain Coughlin swung around in his chair and raised his eyes. It was impossible to tell whose picture he was consulting: President Roosevelt's, General Pershing's, General Marshall's, or Douglas MacArthur's. Or possibly, Nick Train thought, he was communing with his own younger self, the bright young soldier who went to France to whip the Kaiser.

Coughlin swung back to face the others. 'McWilliams, Dillard, here's what I want. Lieutenant, find yourself a swagger stick.'

'I have one, sir.'

'I expected as much. All right. And, Sergeant, grab a clipboard. I want the two of you to inspect the trainees' barracks. I want you to find at least a dozen gigs. I don't care how hard you have to poke around to find 'em. If they're not there, make some up.'

Lieutenant McWilliams's anger was clearly turning to pleasure. Sergeant Dillard kept a straight face. Nick Train made a supreme effort to become invisible.

Captain Coughlin leaned back in his chair and drew in his breath audibly. 'Go slow. Keep those trainees braced. When you finish, you get out of there, McWilliams. Sergeant, you tell those trainees they're confined to barracks except for meals and training exercises. They'll have a GI party tonight. The works. Swamp out the barracks, polish the plumbing, climb up in the rafters and get the dust out. They have a barracks leader, do they?'

Sergeant Dillard said, 'Schulte, sir. Saint Schulte, they call him.'

'All right. You tell him that he's responsible for supervising the party. When the barracks is ready for reinspection, he's to notify you. You'll bring Lieutenant McWilliams back in and reinspect.'

'Yes, sir,' Dillard grinned.

'And tell 'em that we're holding onto their pay for them, they'll be paid as soon as they pass reinspection.' He made a sound somewhere between a snort and a guffaw. 'That's all. Lieutenant, Sergeant.'

They saluted and left.

'Well, Private Train, what do you think?' the Captain asked.

'I think I have an idea, sir.'

'All right, soldier, what is it?'

'May I take this with me?' He filled one of the cups on the tray Lieutenant McWilliams had brought back, then held it up.

'All right.'

Train took the cup with him, back into the safe room. He placed it carefully on top of the safe, beside the cup that had been there when he first entered the room. He studied the cups. They were identical. Of course that didn't prove much. But there was a small Infantry School crest on each of them. That meant that they came from either the Officers Club or the NCO Club, not the mess hall, despite the instructions that Coughlin had given McWilliams.

He sniffed the coffee in the cup he'd brought, then bent over the other cup. Being careful not to touch the cup or its contents, he tried to detect an odor coming from it, but without success. Even so, he thought, even so, he was making progress.

He'd been attempting to recreate Corporal Miller's actions when Lieutenant McWilliams had arrived. Now he resumed that effort. He squatted beside Miller's wicker chair and reached for his coffee cup, the cup that was resting on top of the safe. He lifted the cup, sipped at the coffee, lowered the cup once more and pushed himself erect.

He crossed the room to the door and extracted the padlock key from his pocket.

So far, so good. But Miller had not opened the lock. Instead he had struck the wood and plasterboard repeatedly with his hands, as if he was trying to grasp the lock and insert the key. The key had tumbled from his fingers and clattered across the room.

Why would it do that? Why did that happen?

If Miller was dizzy, losing consciousness, trying to leave the room, he would have done that. He would have opened the lock, trying to get out of the safe room. Of course he would have failed, the outer padlock would have stopped him. But if he was confused, struggling, he might not have thought that through.

With the key lost, lying in a dark corner of the room, his vision and equilibrium failing, Miller would have staggered backwards.

Train duplicated the act.

Two, three, four steps and — Miller would have collapsed into the wicker armchair. Train collapsed, found himself sitting in the lap of a cold cadaver, leaped to his feet.

No, the blow to Miller's head had not caused his death. It was a red herring, designed to direct the investigation of Miller's death — the inevitable investigation of Miller's death — away from what had really happened. He'd have to have Miller's coffee tested, but in all likelihood that was the means by which a lethal dose had been administered.

Train peered into the corpse's face again. If it hadn't been for the blow to Miller's head, any investigation would have found that he'd died of natural causes. Even young men have heart attacks, and the rigors of military life on a man whose former lifestyle had been sedentary could bring on a sudden deadly embolism.

But who had administered the blow to Miller's head, and why, and when?

Nick Train retraced his route from the door to the wicker chair, to the safe, back to the door, back to the chair. Then he stopped, staring down at the remains of Corporal Fred Miller, company pay clerk.

He wasn't an expert on poisons but he'd learned a little bit about them, first in high school and then at the police academy. Miller had apparently realized there was something seriously wrong with him, tried to get help, then staggered backwards and collapsed into his wicker armchair to die. The only mark on his body was the obviously superficial head wound.

What would cause a death like Miller's?

Based on Train's police training, the likely suspect was digitonin, an easily soluble form of digitalis. That would come from a common plant called purple foxglove, also known as bloody fingers or dead men's bells. The victim might well drink it, for instance in a cup of coffee, and not notice anything for as long as several hours. Then his heart action would slow, he would become dizzy and disoriented, lose consciousness and die quietly.

Just as Corporal Fred Miller had died.

Train made his way to Captain Coughlin's office and told the Captain his conclusions. He described his reconstruction of Miller's movements from the wicker chair to the padlock, the struggle with the key, and Miller's collapse and death.

'I don't know what an autopsy will show, Captain. I'm not sure what signs that poison would leave in the body. Maybe none. I'm not a trained toxicologist, sir. But I'd bet my month's pay that a chemical test will show digitonin in Miller's coffee.'

Captain Coughlin grunted. 'Sounds very plausible, Train. And we'll get the right people in to check those things damned soon. I don't think I can hold out on this thing more than another hour or two.' He put his face in his hands and rubbed, as if that would stimulate the blood flow and help his brain to work.

'Great job so far,' he resumed. 'But if that's how Miller was killed, you still haven't told me how the money was removed from the safe. Not to mention — what do you call it in the detective business, Train — *Who Dunnit?*'

'Sir, I'm not a detective. But I have an idea of how the money was removed. I think that Miller was working with his killer. Whoever was his partner double-crossed him.'

Coughlin picked up his cup of coffee

and raised it to his lips. An odd expression crossed his face. He lowered the cup without taking any coffee.

'What would you call that, Train — an inside job, right?'

'Yes, sir.'

Train paused for a few seconds to gather his thoughts. The silence was punctuated by a booming sound. An artillery unit was practicing coordination with an infantry brigade on the other side of the post. The sound was that of a .155 millimeter howitzer.

'Captain, here's the way I think it happened. Miller's partner opened the outer padlock, Miller opened the inner one. The partner brought a cup of coffee with him. Miller thought that was nice. He left it on top of the safe. Miller's partner opened the safe.'

He stopped, then asked, 'Who knows the combination to the safe, Captain?'

'Same people who have keys to the padlock. Lieutenant McWilliams, Sergeant Dillard, and myself.'

'Yes, sir. Well, Miller's partner opened the safe and removed the cash. Then he hit Miller. The wound looked to me as if it could have been inflicted with the butt of a .45. Miller was still conscious. His partner left, taking the money with him. Miller relocked the door from the inside and his partner relocked it from the outside. The idea was that Miller would claim he'd been attacked by an unknown assailant, maybe a masked safecracker who managed to open the safe and get away with the payroll. That would send the CID off on the trail of an imaginary crook from outside, someone who had managed to get copies of the keys to both padlocks, while in fact Miller and his partner had the money.'

'And what would they do with the payroll?'

Train shrugged. 'I don't know, sir. But I have a suggestion.'

There was another boom, another howitzer round fired.

'The first thing to do is check Miller's belongings. No telling what we'll find there.'

Captain Coughlin summoned the Sergeant of the Guard and had a corporal

71

and a private stationed outside the company office. They had strict orders not to step inside, not even to look inside, on pain of court martial. Then the Captain told Nick Train to come with him.

Train was feeling less like a soldier and more like a cop by the minute.

Permanent party had better housing than transients at Benning. Corporal Miller had lived in a tiny room, partitioned in an NCO barracks. Train used a pair of bolt-cutters to open the padlock on Miller's door and then to remove a second padlock from Miller's foot-locker.

The locker contained clean uniforms, underwear, toilet articles, all in inspection-ready order. Boots and shoes lined up beneath Miller's bunk. Civvies on wire hangers on a wall-mounted rod.

The only non-regulation items in Miller's foot-locker were his religious paraphernalia. Rosary, Douay Bible, religious pictures, a couple of saint's medals.

Train was kneeling in front of the foot-locker, carefully examining its contents. He sensed Captain Coughlin standing behind him and turned to look at him.

Captain Coughlin was studying the contents of the locker, as well.

'I don't see anything here,' Train said.

'I do.' Captain Coughlin frowned.

'Sir?'

'You know Miller was a very religious man, don't you?'

'Yes, sir.'

'His most precious belonging was his Missal. He always carried it around with him. But it wasn't in the safe room, was it, Train?'

'No, I'd have seen it.'

'Then it should be in his foot-locker. Not here, is it?'

Train shook his head.

'Where is it?'

'Don't know, sir.'

'How's this, Train? Maybe the old man can play detective, too. It was just a little book, you know. He could have put it in a uniform pocket. Could have had it with him in the safe room. Probably did. It's a long night in there, no companions, no entertainment, another man might ask permission to bring in a radio, or might smuggle in some comic books or magazines. But a man like Miller would bring either a Bible or a Missal and spend his time communing with the Almighty.'

Train struggled to his feet. He was pushing a quarter century and his knees weren't as flexible as they'd been ten years ago.

'You think Miller's partner took the Missal?'

'Yep.'

'But why, Captain?'

Coughlin shrugged. 'Who do you think Miller's partner was, Train?'

'It had to be someone who had the key to the outer lock.'

'Yes.'

Another distant howitzer boom.

'Who, Train? Don't be afraid. Who was Miller's partner?'

'It had to be Lieutenant McWilliams or Sergeant Dillard, sir.'

'Or — who else?'

'You, sir.'

'That's right. We have three suspects now, Train. That's progress. That's real progress. It has to be McWilliams or Dillard or Captain Coffin. Oh, I know what they call me. Don't be naïve.' He paused. 'Three suspects. Don't be afraid to say it.'

He walked to the window. At least Miller had had a window in his room. He peered outside for a long moment. Looking past the Captain, Train could see the patches of snow covering the red west Georgia clay.

'Where do you think the money is, Train?'

'I don't know. Sir.'

'Try. If you were the killer, Train, if you were McWilliams or Dillard or Old Man Coughlin, Captain Coffin, and you had just robbed the company safe, what would you do with the money?'

'I think I'd try and get it off the post, Captain.'

'I think so, too. All right, come on back to the company office, soldier.'

The two soldiers posted outside the company office rendered smart rifle salutes to Captain Coughlin as he and Private Train returned. The Captain motioned Train to sit opposite him, then picked up a telephone and placed a call.

He picked up a pencil and scribbled a few notes, then grunted into the receiver and hung it up.

'McWilliams and Dillard both drove off post last night. McWilliams left around 2300 hours. Returned at 0400 this morning. Dillard left at 2346 hours and returned shortly after 0500. There's no record of my leaving the post, and in fact I did not. What do you make of it, Train?'

'I don't know, sir.'

Train followed Coughlin's glance to a wall-mounted clock. It was well into the afternoon. He and Captain Coughlin had missed the noon meal. Train's barracks-mates would be on the practice range, throwing dummy hand grenades at cardboard targets.

From outside the building, Train heard a familiar voice. It was Lieutenant McWilliams, dressing down the two soldiers for what Train knew would be some petty offense. A moment later, McWilliams strode into the office and halted before Captain Coughlin's desk. He snapped a sharp salute and all but clicked his heels, Gestapo-fashion.

'Sit down, Lieutenant,' Coughlin instructed. 'Good. Make yourself comfortable. Don't worry about sitting next to an enlisted man, you won't catch a disease.'

McWilliams sent a filthy glare at Train.

'Where were you last night, Lieutenant?'

'I was here, sir. In the company office. Catching up on paperwork, looking over training schedules.'

'Right. And then?'

'Then, sir?'

'Then, Lieutenant. You didn't spend the night here, did you?'

'No, sir.'

'Well, where did you go?'

'I went to my quarters, sir. I got a good night's sleep, then I went to the mess hall and met you there for breakfast.'

'Right.'

Coughlin picked a sheet of paper off his desk, fingered it briefly, then dropped it again.

'Gate guards indicate that you left the post at 2300 hours last night and returned at 0400.'

'Oh. Yes, sir. That's true.'

'That's all right, Lieutenant. You're an

officer and a gentleman. You don't have to stand bed check. So long as you're present for all duties, you can come and go as you please. That's per regulations.'

'Yes, sir.'

'Where were you, though?'

'Am I required to answer that, sir?'

'I am directing you to answer, yes, Lieutenant.'

McWilliams had removed his visored cap and was holding it in his lap. 'Sir, I met some friends and enjoyed a social visit.'

'Right. And where was that?'

'Columbus, sir.'

'Broad Street?'

'Yes, sir.'

'What did you do, McWilliams? Pick up a woman in a bar? Do you have a steady girlfriend? Go to a whorehouse? This isn't a Sunday School class, Lieutenant, we've had a murder and robbery here. Where were you last night?'

'The, ah, that one, Captain.'

There was another boom. It was louder than the howitzer booms, but in fact it seemed to be a smaller explosion,

78

sharper, closer to the company area.

'Which one?'

'Ah, the last one, sir.'

'Please, McWilliams, let's have it in plain English.'

'All right, sir. I was at the Cardinal Hotel.'

'Okay. We all know what that place is. I just hope you were careful, Lieutenant.'

'I was, sir.'

The young officer's face was crimson.

'All right. One more thing. I want to inspect your vehicle.'

'Yes, sir.'

'Right now, McWilliams.' The Captain turned to Nick Train. 'Did your police training include checking out vehicles for contraband, Private?'

'It did, sir.'

Train wound up inspecting Lieutenant McWilliams's 1942 Packard Darrin One-Eighty. The convertible came up spotlessly clean and innocent, inside and out. McWilliams stood by fuming, Captain Coughlin watched noncommittally. Nothing under the hood but a perfectly maintained straight-eight engine. Nothing in the trunk but a jack, a tire iron, a tool kit, and a spare tire. At the end, Train crawled out from under the car, dusted himself off and presented himself to Coughlin.

'Nothing, sir.'

'All right, Train. Lieutenant McWilliams, you hurry out to the grenade range and have a look-see. That was a nasty pop a little while ago. I hope somebody didn't set off a real grenade. Train, you come with me. We're going to have a look at Corporal Miller's vehicle. McWilliams, you don't mind if we borrow your tire iron, do you? Just in case we need it to pry open Miller's car?'

But Miller's little '36 Nash 400 had been left unlocked. The True Believer in All Things Holy had trusted his fellow man to that extent. Or maybe he had nothing worth stealing. There was no trunk lid in the odd little car. Train scrambled over the seat to get into the trunk. The car wasn't as well maintained mechanically as McWilliams's Packard, nor was the interior quite as clean and innocent.

Train emerged with a half-empty bottle

of Bourbon in one hand and a stack of ratty publications in the other. 'Girly books,' he grinned, offering the loot to Captain Coughlin.

The Captain grinned and shook his head. 'So little Miller had a pair of gonads, too.' He brushed his hand across his forehead. 'Well, we'll just toss that stuff. No need to upset his family, they've got grief enough coming. No Missal, though?'

'No, sir.'

'Okay, soldier. On to Sergeant Dillard's wagon.'

But before they got to that vehicle, a soldier in olive fatigues came panting up, perspiring profusely despite the winter chill. Train recognized the ruddy complexion and the curly rust-colored hair sticking out from under the man's fatigue cap. It was Aaron Hirsch. He wasn't crying, just sweating.

He managed to pull himself together and salute the Captain.

'Sir, Lieutenant McWilliams sends his respects and a message for the Captain.'

'Yes, yes.' Coughlin returned the salute. 'What is it, Hirsch?'

'It's Sergeant Dillard, sir.'

'What happened?'

'He was demonstrating grenade technique, sir. He had a practice grenade. It was painted the way they are, to show they're not armed. He pulled the pin and counted down to show us how long it took for the fuse to burn. It went off, sir. It wasn't a practice grenade. It was a live grenade. He — it went off, sir. It blew him to bits, sir.'

'Jesus, Jesus, Jesus, Joseph and Mary. Jesus. The poor bastard. He must have known the jig was up. All right, here comes McWilliams now.'

And Lieutenant McWilliams arrived, polished shoes covered with red Georgia dust even in winter, uniform spotless and pressed, every brass button glittering in the December sunlight. Even before McWilliams got off his salute, Captain Coughlin barked at him.

'You've sent for the medics, of course.'

'Yes, sir.'

'Cancelled the rest of the session and sent the men to barracks.'

'Under command of Private Schulte,

sir. A fine soldier, I can see that already.'

'I'm sure of it. All right, McWilliams. Let's have a look in Sergeant Dillard's vehicle.'

They found it concealed inside the spare tire in Dillard's Ford. Miller's missing Missal. The annotations were in a simple code; the Provost Marshal's men and the CID investigators would have no problem cracking it. Poor innocent Miller, the payroll clerk, had made notes to himself in the Missal, notes that gave the key to his carefully maintained records. It was obvious that he never thought anyone would see the contents of the Missal except himself and his God.

Everything was there. The identities of the gamblers, the amounts they owed. The monthly payroll would have got a lot of military men out of debt with whoever held their IOUs. A lot of military men including Sergeant Dillard and Corporal Miller. And Lieutenant McWilliams.

'You, Lieutenant? That's hard to believe. You drive that Packard, you wear custom-tailored uniforms, you're from old money, McWilliams. How could you get in so deep? Why didn't you just ask your family to bail you out?'

'You wouldn't understand, Captain. With due respect to your rank, sir, you really wouldn't understand. I couldn't go to my family. I had to work this out myself.'

Captain Coughlin moaned, as if he and not Lieutenant McWilliams had been caught. 'It was the Army-Navy game that did it, wasn't it? Loyal to the old school, you went double-or-nothing on everything you owed, and Navy whipped Army again, didn't they? You poor sap, McWilliams. You poor, poor sap.'

The Captain drew in a deep breath. Then he said, 'I take it you and Sergeant Dillard and Corporal Miller were all in this together? Who was your bookie? That's not in Miller's book. Was it Jackalee Jennings in Columbus? Or somebody in Phenix City? Big Mike Norris? Larry Sunday? You know, those fellows don't keep their operations very secret, they're pals with the sheriffs on both sides of the river. Who was it, son?'

McWilliams looked angry for a moment

when he heard Captain Coughlin use that last word. Then he shook his head. 'I don't think I should say anything, Captain. Under the Uniform Code of Military Justice I have the right to a civilian attorney and I will ask my family to provide one. That much, I will accept from them.'

'Did you kill him, McWilliams? Tell me that much. Was it you or was it Dillard? Which one of you killed Miller?'

'I'm not going to answer any questions, sir.'

'Dillard is dead now. Very convenient, McWilliams. You can lay it all on his grave. I suppose that's what your lawyer will do, isn't it?' He looked up, looked over McWilliams's cap with its glittering eagle ornament and its polished leather visor. Train wondered what Captain Coughlin saw. He couldn't guess. Coughlin said, 'All right, Lieutenant. Report to the Provost Marshal and tell him to place you under arrest pending investigation.'

Nick Train watched Lieutenant McWilliams salute, execute a smart about face, and march off like a good little soldier.

'Where did they get the poison?'

Captain Coughlin asked. He didn't direct the question to anyone in particular, but Private Train and Private Hirsch were both within earshot.

'Foxglove is common,' Train said, 'it grows in every ditch in the state of Georgia.'

'Lot of it in Spain, too,' Hirsch volunteered. 'I was there with the Lincolns, you know. Saw plenty of foxglove.'

Captain Coughlin said, 'All right, boys, you go back to your barracks and polish your boots.'

THE LADDIE
IN THE LAKE

An eleven-year-old bugler was blowing Reveille while a couple of eight-year-olds, selected for the honor of raising Old Glory, were earnestly tugging at the ropes. The rest of the camp community stood in line for the daily flag-raising ceremony, hands raised in pseudo-military salute. Counselors stood at each end of the line of city kids enjoying their annual dose of fresh air and wholesome athletics at Camp Orinsekwa for Boys, Niverville, New York.

That was when Harry Mendelssohn came charging up the long dirt track that led from the lake to the grassy mound where the flagpole stood. Not that many years past his days as an Olympic water polo star, Mendelssohn grabbed me by the elbow and dragged me away from the hundred-and-fifty or so kids and their not-much-older counselors. Harry was an exception, a muscular forty-something. I was another, almost as ancient as he was, back from the war and happy to dress in blue jeans and a tee-shirt. If I never struggled into another uniform again, it would be too soon for me.

We drew up behind the headquarters cabin and Harry shook his head as if he couldn't believe what he was about to tell me. He had muscles like iron beneath a tanned skin. He was balding and wore a heavy gray moustache. He wore his customary swim trunks, lightweight jacket and moccasins.

'Nick,' Harry began, 'you're a cop — '

'Ex-cop,' I interrupted.

'Okay. You've gotta come with me.'

I started to ask why but Harry didn't wait and he didn't say another word. He hustled me back down the track he'd just climbed. When we got to the lake he pointed to a picnic table that campers used for cookouts. Someone was lying on the table. It didn't take me any time to realize that he was dead.

The male body was clad in pajamas. They were soaking wet. The feet were bare. At first I couldn't recognize the man because his forehead and in fact the whole upper half of his face was crushed in. He looked like some of the corpses I'd seen in Europe during the war.

I've seen a lot, had seen a lot as a member of New York's Finest before Pearl Harbor and as a CID — Criminal Investigation Division — military cop for next three and half years. I'd seen a lot, but I still recoiled from this one. But there was no gainsaying Harry Mendelssohn. He had me by the elbow and he dragged me over to the picnic table.

'Look at that, Nick.' He pointed to the corpse. 'I found him floating in the reeds near the canoe dock. He was face down. I pulled him out and brought him up here before I even saw — ' He paused, then started again. 'I'm going to get Bloom.' He started back up the track. He still had the powerful lungs of an Olympic swimmer.

He didn't have to tell me what he saw.

The lower half of the face was intact. I recognized a nasty scar that I'd seen on this guy before, a scar that ran along the side of his jaw. He'd told me that he got it from a Nazi bayonet during the Battle of the Bulge. He was the counselor from Van Buren Cabin, Camp Orinsekwa's holding pen for thirteen-year-olds.

Every cabin was named for a former President of the United States, starting with Washington Cabin for the youngest kids, the six-year-old innocents, and running through Taylor Cabin, for the seventeen-year-old junior criminals.

His name was Eric MacTodd, known as Scotty for his Scots origins and his rolling burr. He'd been a boxer before the war, he claimed, a tough club fighter in Edinburgh and Glasgow. After the war he'd come to America to make a new start. He was working at Camp Orinsekwa this summer, like me, one of the two token *goyim* in a summer camp for Jewish kids.

MacTodd was — had been — a talented guy. He gave boxing lessons to those kids who were interested and he doubled with Ira Rosen, the camp's theatrical producer, director, and amateur impresario, teaching comedy and music. Halfway through the summer the camp held its annual Parents' Day, and Rosen and MacTodd pulled together a wildly successful camper-and-counselor talent show. MacTodd did a Harry Lauder impression complete with sporran, kilt, and Tam o' Shanter that brought down the house.

It was cold up here at this hour of the morning. Most of the kids wore sweaters and long pants for the morning ceremony, then switched to tee-shirts and shorts after breakfast. I had to show how tough I was, and I shivered, in part because a chilling breeze came off the lake and in part because of what was lying on the rough wooden table.

I made myself study MacTodd's ruined face. There was no question of who he was. We'd sat together the night before, sharing a beer and shooting the breeze with a handful of other counselors after Taps had sounded and the campers were all in bed.

Terry Aronsky was there. A journalism student from Columbia, he was the editor of the *Orinsaga*, Camp Orinsekwa's more-or-less daily mimeographed newspaper. The *Orinsaga's* single page was normally dominated by news relating to the kids — casting calls for stage productions, results of swimming tests, baseball games, tennis tournaments, track and field competitions. Some of the kids could run like the wind. Others were really strong. The *Orinsaga* kept all-time Camp Orinsekwa records for the hundred-yard dash, broad jump, javelin throw, shot put. One of this year's kids had broken the camp record for tossing that sixteen-pound iron ball.

Last night Terry had passed out advance copies of this morning's *Orinsaga*. Among the usual camp news he'd inserted a brief reminder that today, August 15, would be the first anniversary of VJ Day, the day that Japan had surrendered, ending World War Two. That meant that Morris Bloom, Camp Orinsekwa's head counselor, would be making a little speech after the flag-raising ceremony and before the kids headed to the dining hall for breakfast. And that meant that Harry Mendelssohn would find the Camp Orinsekwa community still assembled around the flagpole.

I shook my head. What had happened to MacTodd? There were some pale yellow smudges around the crushed area in his face. It looked like an impact wound. His forehead was smashed in and the bone splinters, all too visible, had punched into his brain. Whatever had struck him had clearly killed him instantly, but there was no sign of what it was.

After a few minutes I turned away from the body, gazing out over the tranquil scene of the swimming area, the diving float and the roped-off crib where pre-swimmers played and took their swimming lessons. I turned around and saw Harry Mendelsson striding down the track. Morris Bloom was puffing along, trying to keep up with Mendelssohn. Shirley Levine, the petite, businesslike camp nurse, was with them. I muttered under my breath, 'Fat lot of good you can do the poor bastard, Shirley.'

They halted and stared at the body. Bloom turned away, a sickened expression on his face. Levine leaned over the picnic table. She touched MacTodd's face with her fingertips, something I hadn't been able to do. 'Cold,' she whispered. She held up her fingers. They were smudged with yellow. She sniffed them. 'Huh, paint.'

Morris Bloom faced us again. He had recovered a little of his usual hearty manner. 'Everyone is eating breakfast now. We'd better get up to the dining hall and put everybody on a rainy day schedule. The kids have to make their beds and clean their cabins after breakfast anyway. That'll keep them there reading comic books and writing letters home while we figure out what to do.'

He started to move toward the dirt track.

Shirley Levine said, 'I think I'd better stay here.'

'There's nothing you can do,' I told her. 'MacTodd is way beyond anything anybody can do for him.'

She nodded. 'Even so,' she said.

Before anyone else could move, Harry Mandelssohn said, 'I'm going to stay with Shirley. Whoever did this — ' He tilted his head toward the picnic table.

Bloom grunted. He started back up the track. I stuck with him. By the time we reached the dining hall the kids were well into their meal of hot oatmeal, scrambled eggs, English muffins, toast, marmalade and orange juice. There were pitchers of milk on the tables and coffee for the counselors.

There were more counselors than there were cabins, specialists in arts and crafts and theatrics who filled in supervising the kids when their regular counselors had their occasional days off. Terry Aronsky spent full-time supervising a staff of ambitious junior journalists and turning out the daily *Orinsaga* and Harry Mendelssohn's waterfront duties were expected to occupy all of his time and energy. Morris Bloom leaned over Terry Aronsky and whispered a few words. Aronsky looked astonished, then pushed his chair away from his table and left the dining hall.

Morris Bloom stationed himself on the platform in front of the tables and blew a whistle that had hung on a lanyard around his neck. The rumble and buzz of conversation and the clatter of silverware and china stopped.

I wondered what he was going to say

about MacTodd but all he did was announce that the camp was on a rainy day schedule until further notice. There were some exclamations of surprise at that, not unexpected as the August sun was bright and the day had already started to warm, but Bloom refused to answer questions. Instead he strode from the platform.

A hundred fifty pre-adolescents and adolescents and college-age counselors have a monstrous cumulative appetite. The buzz of conversation resumed and they went back to their scrambled eggs and English muffins.

Morris Bloom left the platform. He headed for the back of the dining hall, took me by the elbow and steered me from the building.

Outside, the colors seemed super-intense. The green grass, deep blue sky, puffy white clouds and brilliant sun were like something out of a Technicolor movie. A couple of robins swooped overhead, circling each other in something that must have been a mating dance.

'Scotty had Van Buren,' Morris Bloom

said. 'I had Larry Chernov from arts and crafts sit with Scotty's kids for breakfast but they're going to need somebody stronger than Chernov to get them through this. I want you to herd them back to Van Buren and settle them down.'

I nodded. 'You want me to tell them about Scotty?'

Bloom pursed his lips. 'Maybe not.'

'They're going to ask.'

'Tell them he was called away.'

'Won't work. These aren't little kids. They're thirteen. Isn't that a coming-of-age point for them?'

Bloom nodded. 'They've all been *bar mitzvahed*. They're citizens of the House of Israel.'

'They'll have to know eventually, Morris. Their counselor can't just disappear. They're going to find out. Best if I tell them.'

Morris Bloom studied the toes of his shoes, took a couple of steps toward the headquarters cabin, then stopped and looked back at me. 'You're right, Nick. You're a cop, you understand this kind of thing.'

'Ex-cop,' I corrected him. I strode back into the dining hall. Some of the kids had started a song and it spread through the room as if nothing unusual had happened.

Two more weeks of vacation /
Then we go to the station /
Back to civilization /
And then we go to school!

They drew out that final *school* as if it had a dozen Os in it instead of two. Table by table as the kids finished their meal they pushed their chairs back and left the dining hall in clusters. They would head for their cabins grumbling. I hoped that Harry Mendelssohn and Shirley Levine had shown enough presence of mind to erect some kind of barrier at the head of the dirt track and close off the waterfront area. And to find something to throw over MacTodd.

I signaled Larry Chernov and he kept the thirteen-year-old Van Buren kids at their table while I pulled up a newly-vacated chair from the Jackson table and plumped myself onto it. In the rest of the room the waiters were clearing the tables.

I signaled a waiter and said, 'I think these kids are still hungry. Bring us another platter of eggs and muffins.'

The waiter looked puzzled but he obviously knew that something strange was going on and he said 'Okay' and disappeared into the kitchen.

Kids are kids. When they realized that I wasn't going to tell them anything, at least not yet, and Larry Chernov didn't know anything that he could tell them, they went back to their previous topic.

Baseball.

After six weeks of an eight-week camp season, I knew every one of the hundred fifty kids at Camp Orinsekwa. Of the Van Buren kids, Hy Goldberg was a rabid Yankee fan and Stanley Cohen lived and died with the Dodgers. They were arguing about which team had a better outfield. The Yankees had King Kong Keller in left, Joltin' Joe DiMaggio in center, and Tommy Henrich in right. The Dodgers had Pistol Pete Reiser in left, Carl Furillo in center and Dixie Walker in right.

Benny Goodman, the Van Burens'

forlorn Giants fan, tried to put in something about his favorite team but Nadel and Cohen hooted him down. 'Go play your clarinet, you goof!'

'That's just a coincidence and you know it. I'm not even related.' Goodman's voice was just cracking, it alternated between a rumble and a squeal.

At that point the new round of food arrived and the kids forgot their argument and pitched into the eggs and muffins.

When we headed back across the rolling hillside to Van Buren, Larry Chernov went with us. There would be no business in the arts and crafts shed today and he needed somewhere to go. I was glad to have an ally who was old enough to shave.

I half-expected either an outbreak of roughhousing or an organized rebellion once we reached Van Buren and the spring-loaded screen door swung shut behind us, but nothing like that happened. The place looked like the basic training barracks where I'd learned to soldier back in Georgia.

All the cabins at Camp Orinsekwa were built on the same pattern. There was a small porch, a single room filled with cots and wooden cubbyholes, a partitioned-off area designed to give the counselor a slight degree of privacy, and a common bathroom. The bathroom held sinks and toilets. There was a common shower house attached to the headquarters cabin, but with twice-daily swim sessions the kids didn't need to shower often.

Construction was simple wood frame raised a few feet on a cinder block half-foundation. Overhead rafters braced the structure and the peaked roof was covered with tar-paper. The rafters, I knew, gave Morris Bloom fits. They were as tempting to campers as local women had been to GIs during the war. The little kids — say, Washington through Jefferson — couldn't climb them. And the older teenagers — Tyler through Taylor — were too sophisticated to be tempted. But from age nine through fourteen or so — Madison to Harrison — they swarmed up and played overhead like Tarzan on jungle vines. Climbing in the rafters was strictly against Camp Orinsekwa's rules, of course, but that only made the sport more attractive.

To my surprise the kids took off their sweaters and folded them neatly, made their beds in teams of two, checked a duty roster posted outside the counselor's area, swept out the cabin and dumped the trash in a barrel on the porch.

Larry Chernov and I stared at each other. Eric MacTodd must have been a hypnotist to get a dozen thirteen-year-olds to function the way these kids did. A hypnotist, I thought, or maybe a tyrant. They had done their jobs with precision and energy, but they weren't a happy bunch, and when they were done they quieted down more than I thought was natural.

Each kid had a personal shelf above his cot, and they all had pieces of fruit that the kitchen staff distributed every day or so. Every kid but one, Mikey Nadel.

Mikey was a giant by thirteen-year-old standards. He already stood over six feet tall and must have weighed a good two-twenty. He moved slowly but I'd seen him hit a baseball past the outfield so it was lost in a field of wild grasses and never found. He held the Camp Orinsekwa shot put record, and in inter-cabin football games he protected the quarterback, his best friend Noel Epstein, from all comers.

He was sitting on his bed staring at a copy of *Green Lantern Quarterly*. I watched him for a long time. He didn't seem very interested in the story, didn't turn a page, just sat there with a blank look on his face.

I said, 'Mikey, how come no grape-fruit?'

He didn't respond.

'Mikey?'

He laid the copy of *Green Lantern Quarterly* on his neatly made bed and looked up at me.

'No grapefruit?' I asked.

He shook his head as if I'd asked the question in classical Greek. 'Everybody has a grapefruit over his bed except you. Where's your grapefruit?'

He didn't seem to understand me. He shook his head, looking bewildered.

Larry Chernov had been watching the exchange. He joined Mikey Nadel and me. 'Are you all right, Mikey?' He turned toward me. 'Mikey comes into the arts and crafts shop sometimes. He's a nice boy.' Then, turning back, 'Do you want me to take you to the infirmary?'

I nudged Chernov and shook my head, but it was too late to stop him. And it wasn't his fault, he didn't know that Shirley Levine was at the lake with Harry Mendelssohn and the cold remains of Eric MacTodd.

Mikey seemed to understand what Chernov had asked him. 'No.' He shook his head. 'I'm all right. I don't need to — want to — I'm just — I was just thinking, that's all. There's nothing wrong with me.'

The other kids were showing some life now. Goldberg and Cohen had resumed their debate, switching their focus from outfielders to pitchers. Now Goldberg was going on about the virtues of Spud Chandler, the Yankees' great right-hander, who had won twenty games in his last pre-war season and seemed headed to another twenty-win record in this, his first full year back from the war.

Cohen conceded that Chandler was a great pitcher but he preferred Kirby

Higbe of the Dodgers. 'He won fifty-one games in his last three years before the war and he's better than ever now.'

Poor Benny Goodman tried to get in a word for the Giants' George Bernard Koslo, a tricky left-hander, but as usual he only succeeded in getting Goldberg and Cohen to drop their differences and gang up on him.

Larry Chernov gave me a look that seemed to say that things were threatening to get out of hand, and he expected me to take charge and do something about it because he had no intention of doing it.

'Men,' I said. Everybody stopped talking, dropped comic books, and looked at me. I'd used my old policeman's command voice. I hated calling on my old cop skills, I was trying to start a new life just as Eric MacTodd had been, but I kept slipping back into my old cop ways.

'Look,' I said, 'men,' addressing this gang of thirteen-year-olds as if they were adults, 'I have some bad news for you.'

They shifted and rustled and waited for me to go on.

'Some really bad news.'

How the hell was I going to do this? I'd told parents that their sons had been arrested, that their daughters had been raped and murdered, that their families had been wiped out in automobile crashes, but I'd never told a cabin full of kids that their counselor was dead.

There was no other way.

'Eric MacTodd is dead.'

No tears, no gasps. One kid, Gerald Gold, must have been more advanced than his cabinmates. He had outgrown comic books and moved on to pulp magazines. He picked up his copy of *Phantom Detective* and opened to his story. Another kid, Paul Abelson, reached up and took his grapefruit from its place. He started methodically peeling it.

I exchanged looks with Larry Chernov. He looked as surprised as I felt at the kids' reaction to the news that their counselor was dead. Or rather, at the lack of reaction. I could have told them that the Italian government had fallen for the third time this week and they would have shown more interest.

What the hell was wrong with them? Goldberg and Cohen had gone back to debating baseball performances with poor Benny Goodman hovering behind them. Mikey Nodel re-immersed himself in *Green Lantern Quarterly* and Gold buried his nose in *Phantom Detective*. Three or four kids were peeling and eating grapefruit.

Young Sid Metzler, a stringbean of a kid with bushy red hair and freckles, wanted to know if the scheduled volleyball game with the fourteen-year-olds from Harrison Cabin was still on. I didn't know and told him he'd just have to wait and see.

Something . . . something . . . something was tickling at the back of my brain. I came close to climbing the rafters myself, then realized that would be a bad idea. Instead I crooked a finger at Larry Chernov. We exited through the screen door.

Outside on the porch I asked Chernov if he could find a ladder and bring it back to Van Buren. He said sure and scampered away. I'd almost forgot that most of the counselors at Camp Orinsekwa weren't much older than the oldest campers. The seventeen-year-old sophisticates of Taylor Cabin.

From the end of the porch I could see the track that led down to the lake. It had been a couple of hours since Harry Mendelssohn found Eric MacTodd's body. I didn't know how he and Shirley Levine were going to deal with the cadaver, but I could see at least that they had managed to set up a token blockade consisting of a row of folding chairs from the social hall, closing off the track to the lake.

I could see a vehicle parked just outside the blockade. As I watched, Mendelssohn came swarming up the track, dragged the chairs aside, and signaled the vehicle through the opening. The vehicle was the Orinsekwa camp car, a Chevy station wagon painted in the camp colors, the metal parts of its body a forest green, the camp logo, a stylized *C-O* painted on the door in simulated gray wood. The actual wood body of the Chevy, along with the green-and-gray painted metal, was coated with yellowish dust.

Okay. Somebody was acting with a modicum of intelligence. When Morris Bloom had sent Terry Aronsky scurrying from the dining hall he had told him to take the camp car into Niverville and notify the authorities of MacTodd's death. Camp Orinsekwa had no telephone connection with the outside world. Half the kids and counselors were upset at being cut off from their parents or girlfriends, the other half were relieved.

A figure in khakis and a broad-brimmed drill sergeant's style hat climbed out of the Chevy. I wondered if Aronsky had found the lawman in Niverville or if he'd had to drive on to the next bigger town, Valatie. He and Aronsky headed down the dirt track. Mendelssohn set the chair-barrier back in place. I figured that the lawman — he had to be a county sheriff's deputy in that outfit — would ask some questions and make some notes. Then they would load MacTodd into the Chevy and head for the nearest mortuary. They certainly couldn't leave a corpse in the sun, and storing MacTodd in the big refrigerator behind the dining hall was too gruesome an idea to contemplate.

Besides, where would they keep the makings for a hundred fifty campers' next few meals?

Larry Chernov came pacing over the grass, an aluminum ladder over his shoulder. I helped him muscle it through the screen door and into Van Buren Cabin. I had him help me set it up so I could climb almost to the roof. From there I would be able to look down at the upper surface of the rafters.

With Chernov steadying the ladder, I scrambled up. As I'd expected, the dust was disturbed by the passage of shorts, blue jeans and sneakers. In one corner somebody had left a stash of magazines — *Esquire, Laff, Pic, Beauty Parade.* Thirteen-year-olds are wonderful. I leaned over the partition to peer down into the counselor's cubicle like a dive-bomber pilot looking at a potential target.

There was Eric MacTodd's bed. If he'd slept in it last night, it had been carefully remade. The blanket was as taut as the one on an officer-candidate's cot, a white sheet folded down with military precision and the pillow looking as if it had never felt the weight of a head. I could see MacTodd's cubbyhole, his neatly folded changes of clothing and his toilet articles arranged in perfect order.

Nothing surprising about that. But there was a surprise for me on the rafter itself. Just over MacTodd's pillow there were some small stains on the heavy wooden surface. Little more than smudges, they would have been invisible if there had been an accumulation of dust covering them, but they were very recent and there was no dust on them yet. I touched one and looked at my fingertip. Yellow paint.

I called on Larry Chernov to run another errand for me. While he was gone I tried to make small talk with the Van Buren kids but they were reluctant to participate. I'd seen this before. In France an unpopular West Point grad had been blown up by a hand grenade somebody had booby-trapped his field pack with. I was sent in to investigate and suddenly nobody in his platoon knew anything. It was amazing.

The Van Buren kids were acting just the

way that lieutenant's soldiers had acted. Gosh, nobody knew anything, they were all busy doing other things when the loot bought the farm. And none of the Van Buren kids knew anything about Eric MacTodd except he was a swell guy and he always made them toe the line on neatness and cleanliness and it was too bad he was dead but they were really looking forward to their volleyball match with the Harrison Cabin kids.

Larry Chernov stood in the screen doorway and gestured. I went outside with him and we put our heads together. What he told me was no surprise, but now I knew for sure how Eric MacTodd had been killed. And I was almost sure that I knew who had done it. Who was the only person who could have done it.

I had Chernov stand in the doorway to make sure that no one left the cabin, not that there was anywhere they could have run to here in Camp Orinsekwa's rural isolation. I went over to Mikey Nadel and put my hand on his shoulder. I tilted my head toward the counselor's cubicle and led Mikey to it. There wasn't much privacy there, but at least we weren't surrounded by the rest of the campers in the cabin.

How the hell do you start a conversation like this one?

'Why?' I asked him.

At first Mikey tried playing dumb, but I pointed up at the rafter and down at the pillow on Eric MacTodd's neatly made cot. 'Did he bleed?' I asked.

No response.

'Probably not.'

No response.

'Your aim must have been terrific. Either that or it was a lucky shot. No, you're too good for that. It must have been aimed.'

No response.

'Mikey, don't drag this out. I know what happened and I know how you did it. Larry Chernov told me that the sixteen-pound shot is missing from the track-and-field equipment shed. And he told me that you'd been in the arts and crafts shed a few days ago working on some mysterious project involving yellow paint.'

Michael Nadel looked at the floor and muttered something under his breath. I asked him to repeat it. He looked up at me and repeated what he'd said, using words and phrases that I hadn't heard outside of a foxhole in the Black Forest.

'Why, Mikey?'

The screen door slammed and I heard Larry Chernov protesting feebly. I heard footsteps crossing the bare wooden floor of the cabin. Michael Nadel startled me by picking me up and setting me aside. Man, that kid was powerful. Of course he'd been the only one strong enough to pick up a sixteen-pound iron shot and carry it up onto the rafters in the cabin. He'd painted it yellow, kept it on his shelf where it looked like a grapefruit, climbed the rafters last night after everyone including MacTodd was asleep and dropped it onto MacTodd's forehead.

Had MacTodd awakened at the last moment? Had he seen that yellow ball falling? Had he tried to dodge, to jerk his head sideways too late to avoid the sixteen-pound weight that was about to kill him? Or did he sleep peacefully, dreaming perhaps of his childhood home in Scotland, during that fraction of a second it took the shot to drop from Mikey Nadel's hand to MacTodd's skull?

Nadel rushed out of the counselor's cubicle, back toward the door of the cabin. I was fast behind him.

He skidded to a halt, facing a newcomer.

A heavy-set woman stood in the middle of the cabin, surrounded by campers, Larry Chernov hovering uncertainly behind her. She wore her gray hair in a short, severe style. Her features bore a strong resemblance to those of Mikey Nadel. She wore no makeup. Her eyebrows were heavy, wiry and gray. Her mouth was set in what looked like a perpetual frown. A flat gray hat covered the top of her head. She wore a shapeless gray dress. An ugly gray handbag hung from one arm. Her shoes were square, heavy, and graceless.

'Mama,' Michael Nadel cried, 'he knows I did it. Nick Train knows I killed him.'

Mrs. Nadel — she had to be Mrs. Nadel — started to say something but Noel Epstein got there first. 'No he didn't, Nick, I did it. I killed him.'

'No!' Hy Goldberg, the Yankees fan, jumped off his cot. 'He didn't. I did it.'

Stanley Cohen, the Dodgers fan, jumped up. 'No, he didn't. I did it.'

'I killed him.' Benny Goodman, the Giants fan.

'I did it.' Sid Metzler, the volleyball player.

'I did it.'

'I did it.'

In a minute there were a dozen confessed killers in the cabin.

'Mr. Train,' the mother said. She reached past her son and shook my hand. 'Mr. Train. Mikey wrote to me about you. I saw you, too. I saw you at the talent show on Parents' Day.' She spoke with a heavy accent, a combination of German and Yiddish. I'd heard that accent before. It was common among the few German Jews who had survived Hitler's filthy work.

'You're a policeman, Mr. Train.'

'Ex-policeman,' I corrected.

'None of these boys killed the monster, Mr. Train. None of them. These are innocent boys, Mr. Train. My Mikey is innocent. His friend Stanley is innocent. Every one of them is innocent. I am the killer.'

I shook my head. 'I don't know what you're talking about, Mrs. Nadel. Besides, it's impossible. You just got here. MacTodd was murdered last night or very early this morning.'

'I killed him,' she insisted.

I took a step past her and looked outside. Through the screen door, past the porch of Van Buren Cabin, I could see her car. It was an old Studebaker, something out of the early 1930s, its paint job as dull and tarnished and gray as Mrs. Nadel. She had driven it across the campus, bumping up and down hills, and parked outside the cabin where her son awaited.

'Look, I'm not a police officer. That was all a long time ago. I'm just a camp counselor. I think you'd better come with me.'

Larry Chernov stayed in the cabin with the dozen self-confessed murderers. I led Mrs. Nadel past a dozen kids and a young arts and crafts teacher. We crossed the wooden porch. The screen door slammed behind us. We headed toward the dirt track that slanted down to the lake. I could see that the green station wagon was gone. My guess was that somebody had been drafted to drive to Niverville, or Valatie, or Albany if need be, to deliver MacTodd's cadaver where it would receive proper care.

Shirley Levine was sitting at the picnic table. A cool one. I don't think I could have done it. The sheriff's deputy in the drill sergeant's hat was questioning Harry Mendelssohn and busily jotting notes in a flip-up pad. He was using one of those new 'ball-point' pens that are supposed to write upside down and under water. Under the brim of his hat I could see grizzled, iron-colored hair and skin that had been out in the sun for a lot of summers. The deputy was no kid. I wondered if he had been a doughboy in the war against the Kaiser.

Mrs. Nadel touched the deputy on the wrist. Harry Mendelssohn stopped talking and the deputy stopped writing.

'You can stop with the Sherlock Holmes, mister. I killed him.'

The deputy looked startled. 'Who are you?'

'My name is Shulamith Nadel, Mikey's

mother, and I am your killer.'

Still looking startled, the deputy shifted his focus to look at me. 'And you, sir?'

'Train. Nicholas Train, deputy.'

Something clicked. 'Oh, yeah. I've heard of you. Cop, aren't you?'

'Ex-cop.'

'Okay, good enough. You know the drill, Train. What's the story with this lady? What's she talking about?'

'I don't know, deputy. Maybe we'd better let her tell her story.'

The deputy considered that, then agreed. 'You say you killed Mister — uh' he consulted his flip-up pad, 'Mr. Eric MacTodd.'

'Not Eric MacTodd,' Mrs. Nadel said. 'Erich von Todt.' The way she said it, even through her mixed German-Yiddish accent, made the difference in spelling obvious.

'Not Eric MacTodd?' the deputy repeated. 'No!'

'How do you know this, Missus — uh' — he consulted his flip-up pad — 'Mrs. Nadel?'

'I knew him in the camp. He was a Captain. Hauptmann von Todt. He liked me, you know.' She raised a hand and the deputy flinched. I knew the reaction. But she was only raising her hand to indicate her face. The deputy relaxed.

'I didn't always look like this,' she said. A peculiar smile came and went on her face, bitter and wistful at the same time. 'I was very pretty. It wasn't so long ago, only a few years ago. We change. He liked me. It was against the rules but they all did it. He had me brought to his office. He wanted me to — do things.'

She paused as if she wanted someone else to speak, but no one did, not Harry Mendelssohn, nor Shirley Levine, nor I. Finally she resumed.

'I went along for a while. I hated it, I hated him, but I went along. My husband and me, we had a baby. When he was born — it was the same year the Nazis took over — we sent him to my sister in Brookline, Massachusetts. My Michael, yes. My husband was in the camp, and I was there, too. I thought, if I go along with Herr Hauptmann von Todt he might do something for my husband. I thought, we can survive this, we'll do what we have to do, and the war will end, and we'll go to America. So I went along.'

She stopped and spat on the dusty earth, as if clearing her mouth of something filthy.

'Finally he asked for too much. Too much, the Herr Hauptmann. Too much. I grabbed for something. He wore a bayonet on his uniform belt. The Nazis, you know, they loved toys and trinkets and shiny things, like evil birds, like black crows. He wore a bayonet in a scabbard attached to his belt. I grabbed it. I went for him. I got him.'

She stopped and gestured, drawing a blunt-tipped finger along the ridge of her jaw.

'I tried to cut his throat but I missed. I got him here. Here.' She drew her fingertip along her jaw again and again. 'I got him but he got me back. He had my husband brought to his office in chains, and chained to a chair. He made him watch while he did things to me. When he was finished he took the bayonet and he cut my husband. He cut him here.'

She showed us where Herr Hauptmann

von Todt had cut her husband.

'He made my husband watch him do things to me, and then he made me watch while he cut my husband, and while my husband died.'

She smiled again, her expression a weird, humorless grimace.

'Did I tell you, I knew him before the war? Before he was Hauptmann von Todt. When he was Erich der Narr, Erich the Fool. He was a music hall entertainer. He was really quite good. He played the music halls in Berlin and München during the Weimar days. He was very funny. He knew many languages and he could do accents. *Ach*, his French, his English, his Italian. He was so funny. But then the Nazis came and he was no more Erich the Fool. And when the war came, he served his *Führer*. Oh, did he serve his *Führer*.'

Shirley Levine had come over from the picnic table. She put her arms around Mrs. Nadel's shoulders and guided her back to the table. She made her slide onto a wooden bench. Mrs. Nadel couldn't have known what had lain on the table until a little while before.

The deputy heaved a sigh. He lowered himself onto the bench opposite Mrs. Nadel and laid his pad on the table. 'Are you saying, ma'am, that this man, this man who died, this, ah, Eric MacTodd, was really a Nazi war criminal? That he was really Erich von Todt?'

He managed to say the German words with a fair degree of accuracy.

'Yes. He was the man. That's why I killed him. For what he did to me and what he did to my husband, and to how many others? How many others, Mr. Policeman?'

'But — everyone knows he was Scottish.'

'No. He wasn't Scottish.' She exhaled heavily. 'He was a Nazi. He was a beast. What he got was kinder than what he deserved, but it's better than nothing.'

'But — how do you know?'

'I saw. I was in the audience. I saw him doing his Harry Lauder act, his funny Scottish songs and jokes. It was the same act I saw him do in Berlin when he was Erich der Narr. I caught his eye when he came out to take his bow. He caught mine, too. Nobody saw, everybody was watching the stage, but he saw me. He saw me go like this.'

She drew her finger along her jaw again.

'Nobody else saw. But he saw. After the show, I talked to my Michael. I told him who his Erich MacTodd really was. I told him what to do. I planned everything. I told him when to act. Today. Today. The day the war ended. This was the day to act. I wrote him letters about it, told him everything to do. You can see. I know he saves my letters. You look in his cubbyhole. You'll find my letters.'

'I don't know. I don't know. It's too fantastic for me.' The deputy closed his flip-pad and slipped it into his uniform shirt pocket. He screwed the cap back on his fancy 'ball-point' pen. 'If he was a Nazi officer how did he get to England and then to America? It doesn't make sense.'

'You are such a *Narr*, Mr. Policeman. Such chaos there was in the camps, when the Allies arrived to free us. So many were dead. Such chaos there was. I know what he did. He took the clothes from a dead Jew, that's what he did. He told the soldiers he was a German Jew. They let him go. Then he got other clothes and said he was Scottish. He was a soldier, he was a prisoner of war. Now he was free and he wanted to go home. Oh, it was so easy. You don't know, you can't know, Mr. Policeman, it was so easy.'

She stopped and breathed the clean air there beside the clean lake.

'I told my Michael how to make a shot look like a grapefruit. I told him how to kill the monster. I told him to throw the body in the lake. He's a big, strong boy, my Michael. And his friend, I knew his friend Noel would help him. They did it in the night. Then they went back to bed. You look in the lake, Mr. Policeman, look where the monster was thrown in. You dig around a little, you'll find a grapefruit. A sixteen-pound grapefruit.'

Then I said, 'But, Mrs. Nadel, I don't understand.'

She turned toward me. For the first time I saw her eyes. I looked away. I said, 'Everybody confessed. Everybody in Michael's cabin, I was there, they all said they had done it.'

'Of course. Of course, young man.' She put her hand on my wrist and smiled up at me. I looked at her again. Somewhere inside that tired, aged, tormented face I could almost see the beauty that had been there not so many years ago. Almost, but not quite.

'Of course they all did it. What happened to Michael's father, it happened to Noel's parents and his sister. It happened to Hyman Goldberg's grandparents. It happened to Benny Goodman's cousins. It happened to all of them. It happened in Auschwitz. It happened in Birkenau. It happened in Bergen-Belsen. It happened in Ukraine. It happened in Czechoslovakia. It happened to everybody. So they killed him. They all killed him. None of them killed him. None of those boys. None of them. They were all innocent tools. They were my tools. The gun does not know who it shoots. The knife does not know who it cuts. They are innocent. I killed him.'

She stood up and held her hands in

front of her. She knew how to hold her hands to be cuffed.

The deputy stood up. 'No,' he said. 'No. You didn't do it. You didn't do it and those boys didn't do it. I can tell a lie when I hear it, lady. I've been a deputy far too long. I know what happened, and the truth is going into my report.'

He unbuttoned the flap on his uniform shirt and took the flip-up pad from his pocket. He unscrewed the cap from his 'ball-point' pen and made a note, then put the pad and pen away and buttoned the flap on his shirt.

He took Mrs. Nadel's hands in his hands and pushed them down so they hung at her sides.

'You're a liar, Mrs. Nadel, and you know that's a serious offense. It's a serious offense to lie to an officer of the law in his official capacity, but I'll overlook it this time because you're obviously upset. But I know what really happened to this fellow Scotty Mac-Todd.'

He looked at Harry Mendelssohn and at me and at Shirley Levine, the camp nurse.

'Scotty liked a drink, didn't he?'

We looked at one another, then Shirley said, 'He used to come over to the infirmary and we'd have a nightcap a couple of times a week.'

'And he liked a beer or a shot of scotch sometimes at a counselors' poker game,' Mendelssohn said.

I couldn't say anything, I just nodded and grunted my agreement.

'I thought so. All right, here's what happened,' the deputy said. 'He had a snootful last night. That's right, isn't it, Train?'

'Yes.'

'He went to bed but he couldn't sleep. Something was bothering him. So he decided to treat himself to a little midnight swim. He must have been pretty drunk to try it in his pajamas, that proves he wasn't right. He swam out to the diving float and climbed the ladder to the high board and lost his way. He turned around and dived in the wrong direction. Hit his head on the corner of the float. Poor bastard. Knocked his brains out. A fall like that will do it. Knocked his brains out and fell in the water. He didn't drown. He was dead before he ever hit the water.'

He took his notebook out and looked at it for a little while and put it away again.

'Anybody have any problem with that?'

Nobody said a word.

'Okay, then. Okay. That's that. That's what my report is going to say. It was a tragic accident. Proves you shouldn't drink and dive.'

He stopped and laughed at his own joke but nobody else laughed.

'All right then. That's my report, and that's what the official finding will be, or my name isn't Deputy Dougal MacDougald.'

DEADLY RIVALS

'You have to get rid of her!' Linda screamed. 'I can't take any more of this, Arthur! You have to do something about her!'

Arthur Pym put down his heavy briefcase, took one look at his wife, and decided that she would not respond favorably to a husbandly kiss. Not even a token peck on the cheek. 'What now?'

'Arthur, I work hard at my job. I know it doesn't pay a lot, but I make my contribution to this family. And you know this house is mine. And that shiny car you love so much! If it hadn't been for Daddy's money, we'd be living in a dingey apartment and driving an old clunker.'

'Yes, yes, you're right.' He longed for a martini. Something icy cold and sparkling clear, with a tiny green olive in it and just a whisper of vermouth. He wished that he'd stopped on the way home and had one, instead of planning to sip it at home, but it was too late now.

'I work a long day, too. I just got home a few minutes before you did,' Linda said.

He would have to prompt her, he knew. She wouldn't just come out with the story, but there would be no peace until she'd told it, so he forced himself to feign curiosity. 'What did she do this time?'

'I don't suppose you've listened to the tape, Arthur, have you?'

'How could I? I just got home.' He slipped out of his warm coat and hung it in the closet. He loosened his tie.

'Maybe you should hear it,' Linda said, 'but I was so mad, I erased it.'

'Oh,' Arthur grunted. What was he supposed to say to that? If he said he was pleased not to hear the tape he'd contradict her and a tirade would follow. If he agreed with her — was this a verbal trap? He decided to chance it. 'That's too bad, I'd have liked to hear it.'

'I'll bet you would! You just love everything about that slut, including her voice, don't you?'

Wrong!

Arthur managed to edge past Linda and make his way to the liquor cabinet. He got out the cocktail shaker and the ingredients. He'd have been quite willing to forego the olive, but he had to get to the kitchen anyhow for ice, so he might as well have both. An oliveless martini was no great sacrifice, but a warm one was unthinkable.

Linda kept her shoulder behind Arthur's, chivvying him as he carried the silver shaker and the gin and vermouth bottles into the kitchen. She managed to make her proximity a hostile act, keeping inside his personal space, making him uncomfortable.

As Arthur broke ice cubes from their tray, Linda kept up a verbal barrage. Arthur wrapped the ice cubes in a dishtowel and pulverized them with a hammer. The cocktail shaker was cleverly designed. It had a double skin, and Arthur sifted the pulverized ice into the space between the layers. Thus the contents of the shaker itself could be chilled but not diluted.

'There were five calls,' Linda was saying. 'Five, can you believe it?'

Arthur grunted and held the gin bottle

over the open shaker. He had an accurate eye and a fairly steady hand. 'Martini?' he asked.

'Don't change the subject! The first one was supposed to sound like a business call. 'This is Miss Morgan at Acme and Jones'', she mimicked Mae Anne Morgan's voice, ''calling for Mr. Pym. I have an urgent message.' Urgent message my foot! That strumpet! As if you were going to take business calls at home in the middle of the day!'

'I won't take her calls at work, Linda. You know, I told her not to call me either there or here.'

'Then the second one, 'Is Arthur there, please?' Butter wouldn't melt in that bitch's mouth! 'Is Arthur there, please?''

Arthur had to admit that Linda was a good mimic. If he closed his eyes, blotting out Linda's dark hair and eyes, her sharp features and slim figure, he could almost *see* Mae Anne Morgan. Mae Anne was the antithesis of Linda. Blonde, round-faced, buxom.

'Then the other three calls,' Linda went on. 'She just let the tape run and hung up. Just to annoy me. Just to make herself felt!'

Arthur tried to ask his question once more, this time using only his eyes and a little body language, but Linda refused to respond. So Arthur poured enough gin for them both, added a drop of oily liquid from the green bottle, and swirled the concoction gently. He didn't want to bruise the vermouth. He put the shaker on a tray with two glasses and edged around Linda to the doorway. In the living room he put the tray on the low table and poured two martinis. If Linda didn't drink hers, Arthur would.

'She isn't really doing any harm,' Arthur offered tentatively. 'If we just ignore her, maybe she'll get tired and stop pestering us.'

'Don't be a fool! She'll never do that. She's after you, and she won't stop until she has you. Sometimes I think I'd be better off if I just let her have you. Good riddance to bad rubbish!'

'No, no. I'll do something about her.'

'You rutting goat! Are all men like you? They think with their gonads? Or is Mae

Anne that much better than I am?'

Arthur resisted the temptation to make some wisecrack of an answer. Like, *Wait while I try and remember, it's been so long, Linda.* He thought better of that. 'How many times do I have to apologize?' he asked instead. 'I was wrong. I'm sorry I did it. You said you forgave me, that you wanted us to stay together. Can't we forget the whole thing?'

'Not with Mae Anne chasing around after you with her claws out. First she was sending you those coy little invitations. Then the time she showed up on our doorstep — to drop off a parts catalog, of all the feeble excuses!'

'She *is* in the business,' Arthur offered.

'I'll bet she is!'

'She really is, Linda. I wish she weren't. If she hadn't been in Chicago for the convention, this would all never have happened. I wish I'd never laid eyes on her!'

'Too bad that wasn't all you laid on her!'

His hand holding the tall-stemmed glass shook and drops of gin-and-vermouth spattered onto the table-top. He managed to put the glass down without spilling any more, pulled a bandanna from his pocket and wiped the liquid away.

'You are such an easy mark, Arthur. If you were a woman you would have been pregnant by the age of twelve. The boys would have lined up at your door like dogs after a bitch in heat. Do you really think you met Mae Anne by accident?'

Arthur leaned forward and sipped from the rim of his glass. The martini was cold, clear, delicious. Maybe he should have been a bartender instead of a plumbing contractor. No, there was just so much plumbing he could put in his own house — Linda's house — and he had installed the latest of everything. But a bartender who becomes fond of his own wares is in dire peril.

'Arthur! Stop swimming in that booze and answer me!'

He looked at her blankly.

'You don't really believe that Mae Anne was in that saloon by accident, do you?'

'Of course she was. Well, you know, the convention was going on, and everybody heads for the local taverns and restaurants when the proceedings end each day. I just wanted to have a drink or two. I'd been sitting in seminars all day and I wanted a drink, that's all.'

'And Miss Blonde Bombshell just happened to be there, too.'

'Yes.'

'And she just happened to notice your convention badge, and you just happened to notice hers. If she'd been wearing it on her elbow I bet you wouldn't have seen it!'

'Please, Linda, we've been over this a hundred times. Why do we need to drag it all out again?'

'What did you do, ask her about the latest twist in copper plumbing? Or did you offer to buy her a drink? What did she drink, Arthur? Did she have a martini with you?'

'Linda, for god's sake!'

'What did she drink? A Shirley Temple?'

'She drank gin-and-bitters. That's all she ever drinks. We took a bottle back to the hotel with us, to her room. We were going to look at some new product specs.

She *was* there on business, you know.'

'Sure, Arthur.'

'I was wrong. I'm sorry. I was lonely, it was a strange city, I had a couple of drinks too many. I can't undo what's done, Linda, nobody can do that.'

'And Miss Superbosom just happened to be transferred to Vernon City the next month.'

'Yes.

'All a coincidence.'

'As far as I know, that's all it was.'

'And she started coming after you again?'

'Yes.'

'You can't tell me you're not flattered. Miss Big Boobs coming to see you, calling you all the time, trying to get you back in to her bed all the time.'

Arthur had finished his martini. Seeing that Linda hadn't touched hers, he switched glasses with her and started the second.

'Well?'

'Linda, I swear to you, I don't want to have an affair with this woman. It was supposed to be a one-night stand, that's all she ever meant to me. It isn't right, I won't try to justify it, but it does happen all the time, and once it's over that's the end of it. Those are the rules. Everybody knows that. I was just unlucky. I ran into somebody who won't play by the rules. I'd be the happiest man in the world if I could get rid of her.'

There was a long pause. Then Linda said, 'There is a way.'

Arthur looked at her.

'There is a way,' she repeated.

'You don't mean . . . '

'Yes, I do.'

'I don't know,' Arthur said. 'In all the books and movies, you can just hire a hit-man, but I don't know any hit-men. They're not in the yellow pages. I wouldn't know how to find one.'

'Don't they always ask bartenders about that kind of thing?' Linda asked.

'I don't really *know* any bartenders. I mean, I have a drink now and then at lunchtime or after work, but I don't really know any bartenders. I wouldn't know what to say. What if I asked one and he reported me to the police? Even if nothing happened, isn't that conspiracy or something? I'd be afraid. I don't think I could do that. Besides, it must be awfully expensive.'

Arthur wrung his hands. 'I guess I could go down to the Commerce Square project. We're doing the plumbing contract on that, and I know some of the fellows working there. They're demolishing that old hotel, the old Commerce Inn. Then we're going to work on the new structure. I could ask if they have any poisonous chemicals there. They have to do the demolition just so, you know, just to take down the old building they want to get rid of, and not damage the others. Some of the chemicals they use, the explosives and the fusing chemicals and dampers — maybe I could borrow something. I know George Smycowski, the foreman there. I don't know what I could say, but I could try.'

Linda said, 'Never mind George Smycwhatsis, it's all right.' She stood and up and started from the room.

Arthur looked after her. 'All right? It's all right?' Was that all? he wondered. Was she willing to let it go at that?

'No hit-man,' Linda said.

'No hit-man.'

'No chemicals,' Linda said

'No chemicals.'

'You'll just have to do it yourself.' She walked out of the room. Five minutes later she was back. She held a small white envelope toward him.

'What's this?'

'Rat poison.'

'What?'

'You heard me. She won't leave town, she won't leave you alone, and you won't hire a man to get rid of her for you. So you'll just have to do it yourself.'

He held the envelope, staring. 'But — how?'

'How did I get it? Don't be stupid. I just took the bus to the Lakeview District and bought it in a hardware store. It was miles from here. The clerk filled out a sales slip and I gave him a false name and address. They'll never connect some woman on the other side of the town with the murder of a plumbing parts saleswoman downtown.'

Feeling as stupid as Linda seemed to think he was, Arthur turned the envelope around and around. 'But — how do I get her to take it?'

'I'll spell it out, Arthur. Miss Sexpot is so eager to see you again, you call her up and tell her you're willing.'

'I guess I could say I want to place an order for some porcelain goods or something.'

'Believe me, Arthur, you won't need an excuse.'

'But her office — I mean, Acme and Jones is a big outfit.'

'Trust me, Arthur, she'll tell you she left the catalog at home.'

★ ★ ★

As usual, Linda was correct. A phone call the next morning, from Arthur's office to Mae Anne's, brought an invitation to Mae Anne's apartment that very night.

Arthur left the office at six o'clock, stopped for two martinis, and patted the pocket containing the rat poison after every sip. By the time he reached Mae

Anne's apartment, the effect of the alcohol had reduced his nervousness from a violent shaking to a gentle tremor and a cold sweat.

Mae Anne answered the door wearing a thin blouse and tight jeans. Arthur was reminded of the lushness he had experienced in Chicago. He started to stammer a clumsy hello and Mae Anne pulled him across her threshold, reaching past him to slam the door. She reached up to kiss him and he could smell her perfume. Arthur was not a tall man, and he looked down and saw that Mae Anne was barefoot. That was why she had had to stand on her toes to give him a kiss.

'Uh — about that plumbing order — ' Arthur began.

'Who cares?' Mae Anne said. She pulled him toward the couch and pushed him down. She sat beside him and held his hands. A tray of snacks stood on the table, and a bottle of gin peered from an ice bucket. Beside it stood two smaller bottles: vermouth for him, bitters for Mae Anne.

'I couldn't forget your favorite drink,'

Mae Anne purred. 'I think it's perfect that we like the same brand of gin. Martini for you, gee-'n'-bee for me.' She built them each a drink. Arthur sipped his martini. It could have been better, but he had no complaints. The two — or was it three — that he'd had before coming to Mae Anne's apartment were making themselves felt in the form of a noticeable pressure, but he held his ground.

They finished a round.

Mae Anne snuggled a little closer to Arthur. She rubbed her bare foot against his ankle, picked an hors d'oeuvre from the tray, put a kiss on it and popped it into Arthur's mouth. 'You're sweating, Arthur. Why don't you take off your jacket and tie?'

'No!' He wiped his brow. 'I mean it is a little bit warm. But I think I'll keep it on.'

'Whatever you want.' She leaned across him to the bottles, to make them each another drink.

The pressure on Arthur's bladder was becoming a distraction.

'To us,' Mae Anne said.

She hoisted her gin-and-bitters, waited

for Arthur to lift his martini, then hooked her elbow through his to sip from her glass.

'T-to us,' Arthur echoed.

Mae Anne put down her glass. 'I think I'll go and put on something more comfortable,' she said.

'Sure. Uh, while you do, maybe, *ha-ha*, I'll take a look at the plumbing.' He managed a feeble smile.

'Right over there.' Mae Anne pointed. Then she disappeared through a doorway.

Frantically, Arthur pulled the envelope from his pocket, tore open a corner, poured the white powder into Mae Anne's drink, and looked around for a swizzle stick. He couldn't find one and he didn't have time to waste, so he stirred the gin-and-bitters with his finger until the powder was dissolved. Then he ran to the bathroom.

He turned on the water and scrubbed his finger with soap, resisting a crazy impulse to taste the poison mixture before he washed it away. When he was sure he had removed all the poison he dried his hands, relieved himself, then washed his hands again, then dried them thoroughly. He patted his jacket pocket and located the potentially incriminating envelope. He held it over the toilet, found a match and lit a corner of the paper. As the paper burned, the ashes sifted into the bowl. When only the tiniest corner remained, Arthur dropped it into the toilet, flushed it, washed his hands still again, and returned to the living room.

Mae Anne was seated on the couch. She had indeed changed into something more comfortable — a transparent peignoir that left even less to the imagination than her former costume had. 'My, you were gone an awfully long time, Arthur. Are you sure you're all right?'

He perched nervously on the edge of the couch. 'T-to us,' he said again. They hooked their elbows and emptied their glasses. The act of drinking the poison brought them very close together, and Arthur could feel the softness of Mae Anne's body against him.

As soon as the glasses were empty, Arthur felt suddenly relaxed. He said, 'I guess you were right, Mae Anne. It is a little close in here.' He took off his jacket and tie, and laid them across the end of the couch.

'You look tired, Arthur. If you had as long a day as I did,' Mae Anne said, 'well, come on, let's take a little nap.' She looked up at him mischievously.

Could he? Arthur asked himself. Should he? Now that Mae Anne had drunk up all the poison, how long would it take to act? If he left suddenly, might she get suspicious? When the symptoms began, would she call the paramedics? Or the police? How long did rat poison take to act? Had Linda furnished the proper dose?

Assailed by a mob of questions, Arthur Pym decided that his only course of action was to stay with Mae Anne and make sure that the poison had done its job. If she showed any sign of suspicion, he would talk her out of it. If necessary, restrain her until she was — was — until it was no longer necessary.

He let her lead him to into the bedroom.

'Here, Arthur, put your feet up. That's

right. You look so tired. Let me take your shoes off for you.'

He put his head on the pillow. The room was pleasant, Mae Anne's voice was soothing, he *was* tired. And he'd had four martinis, or was it five — or six? — and only a couple of canapes for dinner.

He closed his eyes.

★   ★   ★

In the morning he wakened to a throbbing, pounding hangover. He felt as if elf carpenters were driving brass screws through his eardrums, hoping to meet in the middle of his brain. He sat up suddenly despite the renewed jolt of pain it caused him and looked at the other side of the bed.

Mae Anne was gone!

Was she dead? Had she wakened in the middle of the night and staggered from the bedroom and died on the carpet? Had she gone to the hospital, and if so, were the police even now on their way to her apartment to arrest him, Arthur?

No! There was a note on the other pillow.

Arthur, it read, *I have to leave for work now. Phone me at Acme and Jones, without fail — or you'll be sorry! And don't forget to lock up behind you.* It was signed, *Love, Mae Anne.*

Oh my god, Arthur thought, what now? Maybe the dose wasn't enough. Or maybe it's slow-acting rat poison. Or — he reached for the telephone, dialled Acme and Jones, and asked for Ms. Morgan.

'You fool,' Mae Anne's voice came over the wire. 'What do you think you're trying to do?'

Arthur was unable to frame a coherent reply.

'That drink smelled funny. I decided to risk one tiny drop of it on the tip of my tongue, I know that was risky, but it tasted so weird I poured it in a jar in the kitchen and took a fresh drink while you were making potty.'

How could she speak so freely on the telephone? She must have a private office, a private phone line.

'D-did you — ' he started to ask.

'Don't look for it, Arthur. I took it with me this morning. Had it analyzed. What a dummy you are!'

'Are you going to call the police? Did you drug me? I can hardly remember — '

'No, I'm not going to call the police. And I didn't drug you either. You just got drunk and passed out, you wimp.'

'Then, w-what — ?'

'You'd better get to work, Arthur. Meet me at quitting time.' She named a pub centrally located between their two offices. She hung up before he could reply, but he knew that he would be there. In the meanwhile, he knew that he had to call Linda at *her* job. He didn't know what to tell her.

★   ★   ★

Arthur peered into the dimly-lighted saloon, hoping that he was there before Mae Anne. It was an establishment he'd never been in before. There was a long mahogany bar backed by a mirror. Black leather barstools lined the brass rail. Small wooden tables with red-glass candle-holders on them filled most of the room, and a few curtained booths

155

separated by wooden partitions flanked the open floor.

An old Rock-Ola jukebox glowed in muted colors. From hidden speakers a vaguely remembered Ray Anthony trumpet solo flowed softly into the room.

It took Arthur a moment to get his bearings, as his eyes adjusted from the late afternoon brightness of the sidewalk to the perpetual twilight atmosphere of the saloon. As soon as he had his dim-vision operating, he saw that he had failed to arrive ahead of Mae Anne. She was sitting alone at the end of the bar.

Although the saloon was nearly filled with white-collar types stopping for a quick cocktail on their way home from work, Mae Anne had kept the stool next to her vacant. She signalled to Arthur and he slid onto the leather. Even through the woolen thickness of his winter suit the smooth surface felt cool.

'What a disappointment you are,' Mae Anne opened the conversation.

Arthur said, 'Are you all right?'

Mae Anne shook her head slowly. 'Do I look like a dead woman? My friend, I am not even sick. Although I'll admit, I felt pretty silly after I'd tasted that drink. If you'd picked a better poison, one drop should have done me in. Oh well, we live and learn, don't we?'

Arthur said, 'What are you going to do?'

Mae Anne had a gin-and-bitters in front of her. She picked it up and sipped at it before answering his question. When she did, it was with a question of her own. 'You want a drink, Arthur? Guaranteed non-toxic. Except over the long run, if the doctors are right. What's the old saw? *Name your poison.*'

'I — I don't think I want a drink. Thanks.'

Mae Anne said to the bartender, 'Bobby, a martini for my friend. And build me another of these, eh? This one is nearly gone.'

Arthur was astonished. The bartender hadn't been anywhere near them a moment ago, yet when Mae Anne wanted to order a drink, he was suddenly there. Some people are like that, he thought. Bartenders, doormen, taxi-drivers. Arthur would have sat for ten minutes, trying to get the bartender's attention, embarrassed to make himself conspicuous, getting more and more impatient.

'I, uh, didn't really feel much like . . .' He let his voice trail away.

'Hair of the dog, Arthur. You don't look too great. Hard day at the office?'

The drink was in front of him and he plucked the toothpick from its rim, pulled the olive from it, chewed it slowly. It tasted of salt, vinegar, gin and vermouth. 'You look all right,' he said nervously to Mae Anne. 'I mean,' he leaned over and sipped cold martini from the rim of the tall glass, 'I mean, uh, after last night. I'm sorry about last night. I mean, ah, what I did last night wasn't very nice. What I tried to do lat night, that is.'

'You're sorry?'

He nodded.

'You're sorry?' she said again. 'You tried to kill me, to poison me, and you're *sorry*? You're *apologizing*? I don't believe this.'

'*She* made me do it. Linda did. She knew all about us, she found out, and she

158

wanted me to kill you. She — ' He looked up suddenly. The bartender — it was amazing how one person could serve all the customers at the bar, but he was doing it — the bartender was at the other end of the long mahogany bar, taking orders, pouring drinks, ringing up sales, making change. 'Should we be talking about this?' Arthur asked Mae Anne. 'I mean somebody — ' he dropped his voice still further ' — somebody might hear us.'

'I don't have anything to hide,' Mae Anne said. She tossed off the last of her gin-and-bitters. As if by magic, the bartender was in front of her, asking if she wanted another. She nodded. He turned away, made the drink, placed it in front of her with one hand while removing her empty with the other.

'On your tab, Miss Morgan,' he said.

Arthur had downed most of his martini and waved his hands, trying to get the bartender's attention so he could ask for a refill. The bartender had started toward a heavy-set man in a pinstripe suit with a folded twenty between his fingers, but Mae Anne said, 'Refill,' while tilting her head microscopically toward Arthur.

The bartender addressed the man in the pinstripe suit. 'Right with you, sir.' He swooped back toward Arthur and Mae Anne, mixed gin and vermouth, poured, stuck a toothpick through an olive, placed the concoction before Arthur and was gone again.

'Aren't — aren't you even worried?' Arthur asked Mae Anne. 'I mean, ah, one of us might say something we'd be sorry for if somebody overheard.'

'Nobody pays attention to two people talking in a saloon, Arthur. Don't raise your voice, don't make yourself conspicuous, and we could give each other the formula for the neutron bomb in this joint and nobody would know and nobody would care if they did.'

Arthur said, 'Okay.' He looked around for a bar snack, located a wooden bowl, pulled it toward them, shoved a pretzel into his mouth and munched on it. 'Okay. I guess. Mae Anne, why did you tell me to meet you here? What do you want? It has to be about last night, I know that. I'm right about that, aren't I?'

'You are.' She put her glass down and gave him a hard, piercing look. 'You know what kind of poison that was, Arthur?'

He nodded and made some kind of noise in his throat; he wasn't sure himself what it was.

'Rat poison,' Mae Anne said. 'You tried to dose me with rat poison.'

'It was Linda's idea,' he murmured.

'I believe you. But Linda didn't put it in my drink, Arthur. *You* put it in my drink.'

'Are you going to call the police?' he asked.

She shook her head. There was a blue neon advertising sign against the wall. From where Arthur sat, Mae Anne was silhouetted against the sign. The blue glow, coming through her blonde hair, created a peculiar and morbid halo effect.

'You're angry, though, Mae Anne, I can tell.' Arthur nodded emphatically, agreeing with his own inference. 'You're mad at me because of what happened. I'm glad it didn't work,' Arthur said. 'I didn't want to kill you. Linda made me do it.'

'You already said that.'

'You're mad at me.'

'No I'm not. I don't believe in getting mad. I believe in getting even.'

Arthur felt a chill sweep through him and he put his glass down hard.

'Don't worry, Arthur. I didn't put anything in your drink. Neither did Bobby.' She indicated the bartender, once again busy at the far end of the assemblage. 'No, Arthur. I'm not mad at you, and I'm not out to get even with you. I don't know what made me pick you up at that convention, but now that I've got you, I'm going to hang onto you. In the right hands, you could be useful. But wifey, now — wifey's another matter.'

'Linda?'

'You've got more than one? Of course, Linda. I wouldn't mind so much if she'd tried some other kind of poison, but *rat* poison. *Yuch!* Warfarin! Nasty, rotten stuff! Arsenic, mercury, strychnine, she could have used almost anything. But *rat poison!*'

'What do you want me to do, Mae Anne?'

She stared at him. 'If you were

single . . . ' she said, letting the end of the sentence hang in the air.

'I could divorce her.'

'No good.'

'The house. The car.'

'You'd lose them.'

'This is a community property state.'

Her eyebrow raised a fraction of an inch. 'You bought them? With your joint earnings since marriage?'

'Uh — actually, Linda inherited the house from her dad. And the money we bought the car with.'

'Didn't you know they're exempt from community property, then? Anything that comes from a family inheritance is exempt from community property.'

'I didn't know that,' Arthur said.

'Now you do,' Mae Anne said.

They sat in silence for what seemed like hours. Arthur looked at the clock set in a vodka sign above the bar mirror. He'd been in the saloon with Mae Anne for less than thirty minutes.

'Wh-what are we going to do, then?'

'What *we*, white man?' Mae Anne asked.

Arthur gave her a baffled look.

'Never mind, Arthur,' she sighed. 'I'll spell it out for you in words of one syllable. Your little wifey tried to kill me and I am pissed off about it and you — not *we*, *you* — are going to turn the tables on her. You are going to kill her. You inherit her estate, and then you'll settle up with me. Will you ever, Arthur!'

Arthur covered his eyes with his fingers. 'Oh, my god.' He slid his hands down onto his cheeks, looked wearily at Mae Anne. He said, 'You can't mean that. You don't know what you are saying.'

'I know exactly what I'm saying,' she hissed at him.

'But — to *kill* someone — '

'Keep your voice down, Arthur.'

'To kill someone — someone you hardly know, someone you barely met one time — someone who's never done anything to you — '

'She tried to kill me, you moron.'

The Ray Anthony record ended on the jukebox and out of the corner of his eye Arthur watched the aged mechanism lift the black disk from the turntable, place it back among the other old singles, lift another and lower it to the turntable. Seconds later the sounds of Glen Ray and the Casa Loma Orchestra drifted from the concealed speakers.

'It was your own fault, Mae Anne,' Arthur murmured.

'What?' she exclaimed.

'Well, not exactly your fault, or not all your fault anyhow. I mean — '

'I heard what you said.' She smiled faintly. 'This is really intriguing. Go on, Arthur.'

'Well, only that you wouldn't leave me alone. I mean, Chicago was just one time. You were from another city and everything. I didn't expect ever to see you again.' There was a silence. 'Well, maybe at the convention again next year.'

'And instead I wound up living here, and looking you up,' Mae Anne supplied. 'Hey? You figured you didn't owe me anything, I didn't owe you anything, just a brief encounter between strangers. Is that it?'

Arthur stared into his drink. 'Something like that.'

'This is the modern world. I didn't lose my honor or anything like that. No more scarlet letter. You know what, Arthur? I think you're right.'

'Then we can forget the whole thing?'

'Too late for that.'

'But why?'

'Rat poison, Arthur. Rat poison. Hell hath no fury like a woman who's had rat poison dumped in her highball.'

'What are you going to do then? Are you going to call the police after all? You said you weren't going to call the police.'

'And I wouldn't do a thing like breaking my word. Arthur, if you weren't so fucked up you'd be funny. I still have the poison, you know. I sent it to a chemist I know to be analyzed, but it only took a little bit to test. The rest of it's still there in the lab, along with the test results. Did you wipe your fingerprints off everything when you left my place?'

Arthur pressed his thumb and forefinger against his eyelids and tried to remember. The glasses, the table top, the plumbing fixtures . . .

'You didn't, did you?'

'I guess not.'

'Arthur, Arthur. You really were a mistake, you know it? I'll admit you're pretty good in bed, but anywhere else you're a real dud, you know that?'

He didn't say anything.

'And as for that little cupcake of yours — did she provide the rat poison or did she make you get it yourself? Don't tell me, you wouldn't have had the balls to make up a story and walk into a store and buy poison.'

She shook her head sadly.

'I'll tell you, Arthur. I kind of admire little wifey, at least she has some backbone. But I'm really pissed off at her. Rat poison! So here's what you're going to do for me. You're going to kill her. She tried to kill me, using you as her errand boy — I'm going to return the favor. Only this time it's going to work.'

'What? I mean — how?'

'With a knife, Arthur, with an ordinary carving knife. You do have cutlery in the house, don't you?'

He nodded.

'You won't have to buy anything, you

won't have to make up a story. Nothing. Just pick up the knife and kill her.'

'I can't!'

'Sure you can. You could put poison in my drink, you can put a knife in Linda.'

'But — the blood. I mean — and what if she screams? What if she fights? She won't let me do it. She'll fight with me and then she'll call the police.'

'Then don't let her, Arthur.'

'What — what do you mean?'

Mae Anne looked away from him. 'Bobby, thanks.' The bartender was refreshing their drinks. 'Snack, Arthur?' Mae Anne shoved the fresh bowl of salted nuts and pretzels toward him. 'I mean,' she said, 'that this is really your problem, Arthur, not mine. But if you don't want Linda to fight or scream, you just make sure that you get in one good fast fatal shot before she can do anything about it. Like, sneak up behind her, reach around, and cut the bitch's throat.'

Arthur's skin had turned clammy and he could feel himself shaking.

'Or — here's something even better. Wait until she's sound asleep and get her in the heart. Okay, Arthur?'

He heard himself moan, softly. The record on the Rock-Ola jukebox had changed again, to something by Frank Sinatra accompanied by the Nelson Riddle Orchestra.

'If you think you might not be able to handle that, Arthur, you could hold a pillow over her face with one hand and use the other to hold the knife, to stab her. Then if it takes a little while for her to die, you can muffle her screams.'

There was a ringing in Arthur's ears.

'Don't pass out on me, Arthur.' Mae Anne slapped him hard across the cheek. Arthur heard the blow more than he felt it, but at once the ringing disappeared. He could feel the blood rushing into his face and he knew that he wasn't going to faint after all. He did feel nauseous, though.

Several customers whirled at the sound of Mae Anne's slap, but they saw her rubbing Arthur's wrists and turned away again, resuming their separate conversations. Bobby the bartender hurried over, said, 'Everything okay, Miss Morgan?'

Mae Anne said, 'It's okay. My friend was just feeling a little queasy.'

'Want me to cut him off, Miss Morgan?'

'It's okay. Thanks, Bobby.'

Arthur said, 'I couldn't, Mae Anne. I can't. I mean — a knife. All the blood. Screams.'

'You'll do it, Arthur.'

'But then what? I'll have to call — I don't know. The doctor? The undertaker?'

'Call the police, Arthur.'

'But it's murder! They'll arrest me!'

'Arthur, you'll fake a burglary.'

'But — but — '

'You can do it, Arthur.'

'But it's *murder!*'

'You can do it.'

'I won't.'

'You will. If you don't, I warn you, I'm going to blow the whistle on you for last night. On you and Linda both. You'll both wind up in jail. You do it my way and you'll almost certainly get off. That kind of thing happens every day. Read the paper. You can do it, Arthur!'

He put his head in his hands, elbows

on the polished mahogany, turned sideways to look at Mae Anne. She was perfectly composed, the blue advertising sign halo still shining through her blonde hair.

'When do I — ' he gulped — 'when do I have to do it?'

'Tonight, Arthur.'

'T-Tonight?'

'Yes.'

'B-but, can't I have a little time? I mean, a few days, maybe a week?'

'Arthur, get your nerve up and do it tonight. The longer you wait the worse it's going to be. You'll lose your nerve, you'll say something, do something, Linda will cop to it, that you're up to no good. It won't work. Tonight, Arthur.'

She turned on her stool, took both his hands in hers. For a moment Arthur couldn't help thinking that Mae Anne was beautiful, she was voluptuous, and he knew she was stronger than he was and he had to do what she said.

'Does Linda know what happened last night, Arthur?'

'I — I don't know.'

'You didn't call her today?'

'I didn't call her at work. I mean, at her work. I called home from the office, I left a message on the tape.'

'What did you say, Arthur?'

'I just said that things hadn't worked out last night, and I'd explain everything when I got home tonight.'

'See if you can wipe that tape, Arthur. Get something over it.'

'I could wipe the tape, or even throw it away.'

'That would be even more suspicious. Try and get something harmless over it. The weather report, anything. But if you can't, then you'd better have a story ready to use. It'll be easy. Work out some yarn about tickets for a show or reservations at a restaurant or anything. But have your story ready.'

Arthur nodded. The jukebox was sending the sounds of a Benny Goodman song through the concealed speakers.

'Tonight, Arthur.' Mae dropped her hand into his lap and ran her fingernails up the inside of his thigh. It felt like fire-ants stinging. 'Tonight, Arthur. Tonight.'

Arthur had to try three times to get his key into the lock, but he finally managed to work the mechanism. The night had turned chilly and he stood in the foyer blowing on his hands to warm them after closing the door. He checked his wristwatch and found that it wasn't nearly as late as he'd expected.

He peered into the dining room and saw that Linda had spread a white linen cloth and set the table with her good china. He could smell a beef roast all the way from the kitchen. What a stroke of luck! That meant that the carving knife would be on the dining room sideboard. He found the knife and stood, studying its edge. There was a pleasant scent in the house, even in addition to the cooking odors, and Linda had turned the radio to a classical station so the house was filled with sounds of strings and reeds.

Arthur halted. He'd got an idea. He lowered his briefcase silently to the carpet, removed his jacket and his hat and placed them carefully on the briefcase.

He knelt, untied his shoelaces, and slipped out of his shoes.

He'd once read in a cheap novel that a proper killer held his knife low and struck upward with it, under the rib cage, rather than holding the blade high and striking downward. That way the blade was less likely to bounce off a bone. He would stand behind Linda, call her name. She would turn and he would bring the carving knife up under her ribs and that would be the end of it. No waking in the middle of the night, no pillow over her face, no faked burglary.

He would do the deed, then call the police. Make sure the knife blade was smeared, but if they found his fingerprints on it, so what — it was his knife, he used it every time they had a roast for dinner. He'd got home late, he'd stopped after work for a business discussion over drinks with a plumbing supplies sales rep, and when he got home he found Linda dead. Who could have done it? No signs of a break-in, no signs of a violent quarrel. It must have been someone known to the victim. Was the Pyms' marriage in trouble?

Had she taken a paramour? She might have entertained him while Arthur was at his meeting, the illicit lovers quarreled, then man picked up the knife and . . .

The music on the radio ended an announcer identified it as Mozart's symphony number 40, the *Jupiter*. A commercial began for an expensive brand of imported luxury cars.

Arthur advanced through the kitchen doorway, his stockinged feet utterly silent.

He stood behind Linda, gathering his nerve to call her name. She was standing at the electric cooktop, sauteing onions.

He said, 'Li — '

She whirled, swinging the heavy iron pan. Arthur stood paralyzed as the black pan described an arc, rising from the cooktop, slices of onions and drops of melted butter flying through the air. The frying pan came down edge-first against his skull. He heard more than felt the sickening thud of impact. He didn't even feel the carving knife as it tumbled from his suddenly nerveless fingers, described a perfect flip in mid-air and embedded itself point-first in his stocking-clad foot.

'Talk about incompetence!'

'I know, I know. I mean, you give a guy a simple assignment and he can't do *anything*.'

'Well, he put the poison in my drink. He did that okay. Maybe the flaw was in the plan, not the execution.'

'Are you saying it was *my* fault, Anne Mae?'

'Mae Anne.'

'Oh, yeah. I always think of it as Anne Mae — Anne may, and if you give her a chance she will!'

'Not funny, Linda.'

'I'm sorry. I didn't mean to hurt you.'

'You didn't.'

'I mean, he doesn't amount to much, but he's mine.'

'Uh-huh.'

'And along you come with your blonde hair and your big boobs and — ' Linda reached into her purse and pulled out a handkerchief and wept into it.

'Don't cry, honey.' Mae Anne put her hands on the back of Linda's comfortingly. Bobby poked his head inside their booth and asked if they were ready for a refill. Mae Anne said they were and he disappeared to make their drinks. It was an off hour, the late lunch crowd had finally dragged their tails back to their offices and the quitting-time rush hadn't started yet. In fact, Mae Anne and Linda were the only customers in the place. That wouldn't last, but it was the situation for the moment, and they both had settled into a the seclusion of a quiet, curtained booth.

Mae Anne had fed a fistful of coins into the Rock-Ola jukebox, and Billie Holiday's voice was coming from the speakers.

'You've got the son of a bitch. I had him for one night — '

'Two.'

'The second one doesn't count. He passed out on me. After trying to kill me. If he'd had any sense, he would have held back on the juice and tried to get *me* snookered before he dumped the powder in my glass. That's why I think your plan was the pits, Linda.'

'I thought he could bring it off. I guess I counted on him having too many brains.'

'Besides, you know, you can talk about big boobs and all, but in fact I really envy you. You've got the kind of figure I always wanted, and I haven't had since I was twelve. What size dresses do you wear anyhow?'

'Five.'

'Oh, Jesus! Size five!' Mae Anne stuck her head out of the booth. 'Bobby! A double! In fact, make me a pitcher and bring it, will you?'

'You know, that was pretty bitchy of you to send him after me with a knife. Right there in my own kitchen! I mean, I work hard all day, and then I come home and set the table and put a roast in the oven and slice up all those onions. You know, I was crying before I even cut into one, and then when I got started I couldn't stop.'

'I'm sorry, Linda. I'm really sorry. He was supposed to do it in the night, when you were sound asleep. Pillow on the face, blade between the ribs, you'd never know what hit you.'

'Thanks a million, Mae Anne.'

'Well, you tried to kill me first, Linda!'

'Okay, I guess you had a right. We're even now?'

'Even.'

They shook hands.

Bobby brought them two pitchers, one of martinis, one of gin-and-bitters.

'I don't see how you can stand the taste of bitters.'

'I hate vermouth worse.'

There was a long silence, punctuated only by the voice of Billie Holiday, pain in its every note.

'Linda, what are we going to do with Arthur?'

'I don't know.' She shook her head.

'I do.'

'What?'

'Kill the bastard!'

'Oh, no! How could we do such a thing? That would be *murder*!'

'You bitch! It wasn't murder to try and poison *me*?'

'Well, but you were — '

'The other woman, right. Trying to steal your man. The crime of passion. The unwritten law.'

'Well, you tried to make him stab me.'

'Let's not go around this again, all right?'

Linda bit her lip. 'All right, Mae Anne.'

She toyed with her glass, letting the sound of Billie Holiday flow around her. She smiled at her companion. 'You know, it *is* an idea.'

'It's a god damned *good* idea, sister!'

'But how can we do it?'

'Where is he now? I thought he was supposed to meet us here after work.'

'Well, his foot, you know. And his head. He isn't moving so well right now.'

Mae Anne laughed. 'Serves the bastard right! I can't wait to see him!'

'He was out of the office when I called him the first time. I think he was over at that Commerce Square project talking about their plumbing. He has a friend there, George Something-or-other.'

'Big deal.'

'But he called me back. He's really very contrite, you know.'

'He ought to be. Okay, look here, Linda, I don't know what you saw in the guy.'

Linda blushed. Staring into her martini glass she said, 'We were classmates in school. It was just a date but we got carried away and, well, one thing led to another, and — and I missed my next period and I panicked and — '

'Say no more.'

'I wasn't even pregnant, it turned out. But there we were, married and — '

'Say no more.'

'What did *you* see in him, Mae Anne?'

Mae Anne laughed. 'In a funny way, it was almost the same thing. There I was in Chicago, all alone at this ridiculous plumbing convention. I mean, can you imagine what it's like to be locked in hotel with 4,000 damned *plumbers*, honey, and you tell yourself that this is it, baby, this is your life, Mae Anne Morgan? So I picked up the first male that didn't look like a garbage dump or smell like a Hell's Angel.' She laughed bitterly.

The curtain was pulled back and Arthur stood there. He had a thick white bandage on his head and his foot was wrapped and packed and he was leaning on a crutch on that side, his battered briefcase in his other hand.

'I — I'm sorry I'm late,' he said. 'C-can I sit here?'

Linda started to slide over to make room for him in the booth.

'I don't think we quite finished our last topic,' Mae Anne said. 'Maybe you should take a little hike, Arthur, and then come back.'

Arthur hesitated, balancing on his one good foot and his crutch. He'd lowered his briefcase to the floor. 'Ah, I guess, ah, but my foot is kind of painful. And my head.'

'Come on, Mae Anne.' Linda slid from the booth to her feet. 'I have to visit the powder room anyway. We can talk there.'

'Okay,' Mae Anne assented. 'I could stand a little trip to the can myself.'

They brushed past Arthur, one on either side.

He stood watching until the curtain that covered the alcove concealing both restrooms swung back into place. Then he picked up his battered briefcase and limped painfully toward the street.

★ ★ ★

The explosion ripped out the plumbing in both restrooms, demolished the entire rear half of the saloon, and totally destroyed a magnificent Rock-Ola jukebox. It would also undoubtedly have caused many casualties if it had come at a time when the establishment was busier.

As it was, only two female customers who had the misfortune of being in the ladies' room were killed. The explosive device had apparently been placed beneath the toilet there, and when the handle was depressed to flush the toilet — *ka-boom!*

Bobby the bartender, busy setting up for the late afternoon rush, suffered a broken arm and multiple cuts and bruises.

Arthur Pym, hobbling painfully on the sidewalk just outside the front door, was thrown to the ground. He was not seriously injured, although he bled spectacularly from a number of shallow cuts caused by flying glass.

Even so, as he lay on the sidewalk a few feet from his crutch and his briefcase, Arthur murmured, 'Thank you, George.' But none of the passers-by who came running, their attention captured by the explosion and their curiosity by the sight of the demolished saloon and the injured man, made out the words — or would have understood them anyway.

STREAMLINER

The lonely wail of a steam locomotive echoed across the moonlit prairie. Tall saguaro cactus cast frighteningly human-looking shadows in the bright January moonlight. The train had left Chicago in the midst of a driving snowstorm, the worst that city had experienced in a decade. Now, as it roared across the Arizona desert, the light of a full moon and a million stars reflected off the bellowing behemoth.

The war was over and nearly two years had passed. The nation had welcomed its millions of uniformed heroes home, thanked them for their service, and sent them back into the teeming streets of its cities and the lush fields and pastures of its farms.

Time to earn your way as civilians once again, boys. If the jobs just aren't there, if the horrors you lived on the beaches of Normandy and in the caves of Iwo Jima haunt your dreams like bloody phantoms, well, you'll get over it. Just smile and accept the thanks of a grateful nation.

The hour was late, very late. Almost all the passengers had retired for the night, the well-to-do in their private compartments, the middle-class in folding berths, those less fortunate slouching in their seats, hoping to catch a few hours of shut-eye before the desert sun came glaring over the horizon.

By this time the club car should have been darkened, too, but a few neatly folded bills, discreetly passed across the polished hardwood to a receptive bartender, had persuaded him to stay open for a handful of carefully selected customers.

Two of them were perched on tall barstools. Seen from the rear, they could have passed for brothers. Or perhaps for professional colleagues, on their way to a convention of clergymen.

Or undertakers.

Each was dressed in a black suit, elegantly tailored and maintained with care. Each wore a pair of black shoes, polished to a brilliant shine. Perhaps oddly, each also wore a black fedora. Most passengers remove their hats to ride in trains, but who are we to criticize, eh? Leave them to their foibles.

The two men had been drinking separately when the club car manager sent most of his customers on their way for the evening. Some had drunk discreetly. Others were — how shall I put it — let's say they were feeling no pain. But what harm was there in getting a little bit tipsy, maybe more than a little bit tipsy, while heading toward Los Angeles on the Desert Cannonball? Nobody was going to drive into a lamppost, that's for sure.

Finding themselves the only customers left at the bar, the two men struck up a conversation. Well, there's no harm in that. A couple of lonely souls, happy to have someone with whom to while away the hours.

Names were a problem, but only a small one. One man asked the other to call him Whistler.

'As in James McNeill Whistler?' asked his new acquaintance.

'No. It's a nickname I got because of a little habit I picked up a long time ago.' He paused and whistled an eerie tune. It wasn't exactly pretty, but the other found that it lodged, somehow, in his brain. A very odd melody, melancholy, haunting, as if it would draw you in and keep you there — somewhere — whether you wanted to stay or not.

'You see?'

The other man said, 'Yes.'

'That's why they call me — Whistler.' He paused to sip his beverage, the ice cubes clinking softly with the swaying of the train. 'And you?'

'Traveler.'

'Just Traveler?'

'Yes. Some people think there's something mysterious about that, but most simply accept it. I hope you will, Mr. Whistler.'

'Just Whistler.'

Their conversation was interrupted by a white-jacketed porter clearing away the remnants of the evening's business. Ashtrays were emptied, glasses and bottles were removed from tables and carried to the bar to be washed. Abandoned magazines and newspapers were gathered up.

One of the dark-suited men asked the

porter to leave a newspaper with him. It was a copy of the Chicago *Tribune*, the self-styled World's Greatest Newspaper. He spread it on the bar and scanned the headlines. Chicago was still reeling from news of the death of Al Capone at his winter home in Florida. Chicagoans who had quailed in terror at the violence of Capone's mobsters two decades earlier now felt a strange nostalgia for the brutal mobster. In international news a Frenchman named Henri Verdoux was suing the producers of the Chaplin film *Monsieur Verdoux* that portrayed its eponymous character as a serial murderer. Closer to home the police promised a prompt arrest in the daring daylight robbery of the Farmers and Cattlemen's Bank on State Street. And on the sports page, fans of both the White Sox and the Cubs were beginning to stir in anticipation of the coming baseball season.

From behind the two men came the sound of a woman's voice. 'Hey, up there, can a lonely lady get a nightcap or is this joint closed for business?'

The lighting in the club car was dim,

supplemented by the almost daytime glare of a full moon reflected off the sere sands of the southwestern desert.

The bartender, unobtrusively manning his station, rasped his reply. 'I'm sorry, Miss, club car is closed for the night.'

He winked at his two male customers. 'I see you're checking out the headlines,' he growled. 'What do you think of that bank robbery? Take a gander at that, will ya?'

With a blunt finger he traced the story's subheads. 'Looks like the coppers put a couple of slugs into one of them muggs, even if his buddies managed to drag him into their getaway wagon.' He shook his head. 'Takes all kinds, don't it? That's what I always say, it sure takes all kinds.'

The woman's voice cut in again. 'I don't see you shutting down those two muggs.' She stood up, holding the table-edge to steady herself as the car lurched, jerking a thumb at Whistler and Traveler.

The two men in black exchanged a knowing glance. One of them addressed the woman. 'Didn't you get on the train in Chicago, Miss?'

'Yeah. That's home. So what?'

'Oh, nothing. Nothing at all,' the second man in black replied. 'Chicago is a splendid metropolis. What did that poet call it, 'Hog butcher for the world'? Of course, the winters can be difficult. Are you headed for a warmer locale?'

The car lurched again, and the woman stumbled, caught herself, then made her way forward.

'Here now,' a man in black said, 'won't you have a seat?' He slid courteously aside and the woman climbed onto a red leather stool between those occupied by the two men.

She looked from side to side. 'You two must be brothers or something.'

'You might say as much.'

'You even drink the same kind of booze.' She flicked her deep eyes toward the bartender. 'I'll have the same as the brothers here.'

The bartender cast a glance at one of the men, caught an almost imperceptible nod in return, lifted a silver-capped bottle and a small glass and poured.

The woman gazed into the glass, not

touching it. She turned on her barstool to scan the moonlit desert. Windows had been opened on both sides of the car, and the cool night air of the Southwest provided refreshing relief to the usual stuffy air of railroad cars.

Black shapes flitted through the night outside the car. The woman made an odd gesture, the dark red of her long, pointed fingernails reflecting in the overhead lamps. Something silent and black flittered through the window. It hovered briefly near the ceiling, then flapped its wings, crossed the car and disappeared out the other side of the car.

'Wha — what was that?' the bartender gasped.

'Just a bat.' The woman smiled at the red-jacketed server. She was small and slim, her skin pale and her features fine, a marked contrast to her rough speech. In the artificial light of the club car her platinum-blonde hair, artfully darkened eyebrows and lashes and vivid lip rouge made a dramatic image. A tiny purse of gold lamé hung from one shoulder by golden chains as fine as angel's hair.

The red-jacketed bartender shook his head. 'Pretty weird, but we get 'em now and then on this run. Some women are scared, think they'll get caught in their hair or something.' He gave a nervous laugh. 'Maybe they're afraid of vampires.'

'No,' the woman said, 'I'm certainly not afraid of bats. I use them in my work. And there are no vampires. No human ones, anyway. My poor uncle raised on horror movies, he always believed in vampires. Lot of good it did him, the old fool.'

The train's whistle punctuated her words, its shrill wail echoing through the night.

She lifted her glass. 'To Chicago.' She paused.

'I'll drink to that,' one of the men said.

The woman said, 'Let me finish. To Chicago, goodbye, you've seen the last of Satin Blaine.' She drew the glass to her lips and drained off half its contents. To her newfound companions she said, 'How come you two aren't drinking?'

In unison the two men lifted their glasses. A moment later one of them said, 'That was quite a trick, Miss Blaine. It is

Miss Blaine, isn't it? Yes. Quite a trick getting that bat to fly through the car.'

'I've always been good with animals.'

'And you're leaving Chicago because of the climate?'

She let out a quick, harsh laugh. 'You might say that.'

'Too cold for you?'

'Maybe. Or maybe too hot.'

She took another sip of her beverage. 'Actually, I'm taking my uncle to Los Angeles.'

'Oh. I thought you were travelling alone. I didn't see any companion with you.'

'He's back in the baggage car.'

The lights in the club car flickered, as they often do on trains. In the momentary darkness the bright moonlight pouring through the club car's window settled on the woman's hand. A magnificent Australian opal mounted in a fine gold setting graced her finger; the stone seemed to capture the moonlight and glow with its swirling effulgence.

The electric lights came back on.

'He's dead,' Satin Blaine explained.

'It must be difficult, travelling with a casket.'

'I can handle a stiff. They never give me

any trouble. I've had a lot more grief from live men than from dead ones, you can believe it.'

She heaved a sigh, a world-weary gesture for one so young and attractive.

She downed the last of her drink, lowered the glass to the bar and slid from the stool to her feet. 'Okay, gents, many thanks for the companionship and the refreshments. I think I'll be on my way now.'

'We'll walk you back to your compartment, Miss Blaine.' One of the men slapped a bill on the bar. They both joined the woman.

'Well, how nice of you. But call me Satin, then, if we're going to be friends.'

They left the club car and started toward the rear of the train only to be stopped by a uniformed conductor. His hair beneath his uniform cap was steel gray. His eyes held the look of one who has seen everything there is to see, or who thought so until now.

'Sorry, folks, passageway's closed for a little while.'

'What happened?'

'I'm sorry, you'll just have to stay in

your compartments. Everything's all right.'
The way he said it indicated that everything was not all right.

One of the men in black leaned over and whispered a few words to the conductor. At the same time he pulled back his carefully tailored suit jacket and showed something to the railroad man.

There was a moment of silence. It was broken when the train lurched and the lights flickered.

After a moment the lights blazed again and the conductor nodded. 'Okay, follow me.'

They made their way through a series of Pullmans and ordinary passenger cars. A seeming eternity later they approached the streamliner's baggage car, only to be halted in their tracks by a frightful sight.

A gray-haired oldster wearing railroad man's overalls staggered toward them, an expression of fright on his face. 'It — it — it's a va-vamp — ' escaped his blue lips. His eyes were open wide. He pitched forward and lay motionless in the corridor.

The conductor bowed over the body,

turning it over so that the gaping mouth and frightened eyes stared sightlessly at the ceiling. After a moment the conductor knelt and a uniformed sleeve stretched toward the old man's throat. Experienced fingers felt for a pulse that was not there.

The conductor looked up at the two men in black and the slim, platinum-blonde woman. 'He's dead,' the conductor gasped. And after a moment he added, 'And he's cold. As cold as ice.'

The woman, Satin Blaine, spoke in her distinctive voice, 'He tried to say something. He said, 'Va-vamp'.'

A man in black said, simply, 'Yes.'

Satin Blaine resumed, 'Do you think he was trying to say, *vampire?*'

Briefly, no one spoke.

And what do you think, dear reader? Was the old man talking about a vampire? Perhaps he'd seen one movie too many, or read one tale more than was good for him, about Transylvanian counts with courtly manners and very sharp fangs. Perhaps he was the victim of his own, too-vivid, imagination. Or . . . perhaps not.

We shall see.

One of the men in black asked the conductor, 'Who is this?'

'Old Jenkins. Old Ollie Jenkins. He's been with the railroad for forty years. Started as a fireman and worked his way up to brakeman and finally engineer. One of the best. He never married, never had a family or even many friends. Said he loved his locomotives and that was all the love he needed. Management tried to retire him years ago, but he loved the trains so much, he wouldn't let go. Said he wanted to die riding the rails, so they gave him a job as a baggage car attendant, paid him as much salary as his pension would have been. Can you imagine, a top-notch engineer, sitting and watching baggage hour after hour? But Ollie said he'd do anything he had to, just so long as he could keep riding the high iron. Well, I guess he got his way. Poor old-timer.'

'Enough sentiment,' said a man in black. 'Just a moment.' He bent and touched the white cheek, then rose. 'Cold, all right.'

Satin Blaine asked, 'What could have killed him?'

The conductor shook his head. 'No

way to tell, but it looks to me as if he died of shock.'

A man in black — the one who called himself Traveler — said, 'I need to look in that baggage car.' He stepped away from the others and tried the door. 'It's locked.'

'Baggage car's always locked.' The conductor stepped forward. He pulled a huge key ring from his uniform pocket and found the correct key. 'Even scared as he was, Ollie slammed the door behind him coming out.'

Traveler held up his hand. 'Just a minute, then. Don't be so fast to open the door to the baggage car.'

He turned and placed the palm of one hand on the metal surface, then snatched his hand away as if he'd placed it on a red-hot stove. At the same moment a trickle of white smoke, or what appeared to be white smoke, crept through the keyhole.

An expression of fear contorted the conductor's features. 'Something's burning in there! We'll have to uncouple the baggage car.'

'No.' Traveler held his hand at shoulder level, rubbing it with the other. 'Take a look at Jenkins there.' He pointed at the cadaver. 'Look at his eyebrows, his moustache. That's frost.' He swung around and pointed in the other direction. 'Not smoke, not smoke at all. There's something freezing cold in there.'

Whistler pressed his fingertips briefly to the door. 'You're right, Traveler.' Then he addressed himself to the railroad man. 'Conductor, what are you carrying in this baggage car?'

The conductor reached inside his uniform jacket. 'I've got the manifest right here.'

He opened a small, much-battered leather portfolio that resembled an oversized wallet, pulled from it a folded sheet of oversized foolscap and spread it for them all to see. He ran a finger down a column of brief, blue-inked entries.

'You see? Nothing but the usual passengers' luggage, a few trunks being shipped by express service, and — and a coffin holding human remains. We need a special permit to carry human remains. I've got it right here.'

A second sheet bore official seals and

signatures. It listed the point of origin and destination of one casket, bronze. *Point of origin, Blaine Chemical and Pharmaceuticals Corporation, Chicago, Illinois. Destination, Blaine Works West, Los Angeles, California. Contents of casket, embalmed and preserved remains of Walter Martin Blaine, deceased.*

'Your uncle, Miss Blaine?' Whistler frowned at the shapely platinum blonde.

From her gold lamé purse she produced a lace handkerchief and dabbed at her eyes. 'Yes. My Uncle Walter. My parents both died when I was a child and Uncle Walter was like a father to me. And now, now he's gone.'

The conductor raised his uniform cap and scratched a thatch of salt-and-pepper hair. 'I just don't get it. You have my sympathy, Miss Blaine, you truly do. But I don't see how that connects with this icy mystery.'

Traveler asked a question. 'Could there be any machinery or chemicals in there?'

The conductor shook his head. 'Not possible, sir. Anything like that would have to ship on a freight. We don't mix freight with passengers, not policy, sir, no way. Would be against railroad rules and government regulations both. And even if we made an exception, maybe some high-priority defense materials that couldn't wait for the next freight, why, you see — ' He held the baggage manifest in one hand and slapped the page with the back of his other hand. ' — you see, it would show on the manifest. It just isn't here, sir. It's impossible.'

A pretty puzzle, don't you think? When you have eliminated the impossible, whatever remains, however improbable, must be the truth. *Didn't a great detective once say that? But what happens when you eliminate the impossible — and no other explanation remains? What then, eh? Maybe the impossible is true after all.*

Or is it?

'All right,' Traveler hissed. 'Whatever killed Oliver Jenkins is inside that baggage car. And whatever it was, we're going to find out. Let me have your key, conductor.'

The railroad man had dropped his keys back into his pocket. Now he found them again and handed them to Traveler. 'That's the one. Right there. That's the one that opens the baggage car.'

Traveler held out his hand.

The conductor laid the collection of keys in Traveler's palm. He pointed to an old-fashioned, oversized blue steel key of a type that had been popular half a century before. 'That's the one, sir. That's the one that will open the lock.'

Traveler extended his arm, moving the huge key toward the lock that stood between them and the baggage compartment. Even as he did so the cold white mist continued to pour from the keyhole. Once through it crept down the door like a living, malevolent thing and puddled on the compartment floor, forming a lake of white, icy vapor.

As the key made contact with the lock, a woman's voice, angry, authoritative, maybe a little bit desperate, rang out.

'Go ahead, Traveler. Open the door. And when you do, we're all going to take a ride in the baggage compartment.'

Traveler and Whistler were calm but the conductor showed his puzzlement.

'What do you mean? What — oh.' He nodded slowly, his gaze fixed on the tiny pearl-handled .22 that she had pulled from her purse. It was pointing at them now.

Satin Blaine swung the little automatic from one to another, covering Traveler, Whistler, and the conductor in turn.

Traveler inserted the key in the heavy, old-fashioned lock. He turned it and the lock emitted a loud click.

'Go ahead,' Satin Blaine ordered. 'All three of you, into the baggage car. And don't try any tricks. I suppose you two mystery men are willing to risk your lives but I don't think you'd risk the life of an innocent man. So any tricks and the conductor gets it. A .22 only makes a little hole but if it's through the heart or the brain, it's as deadly as a cannon.'

Traveler shoved the door open with a black-clad shoulder. There was a rush of white vapor as the door swung back. The vapor flooded the platform where Satin Blaine and the others stood, then was swept into the Arizona night as the wind caught it.

One black-clad figure, then another stepped across the platform into the baggage car. Hesitantly, the conductor followed. Finally Satin Blaine followed them, her little gold lamé purse swinging from its glittering chain and the pearl-handled automatic steady in her fist.

Whistler looked around the car. Its contents were utterly uninteresting. For the most part they were men's and women's suitcases doubtlessly containing light clothing for wear in the balmy winter weather of Southern California. There were several steamer trunks. Most likely they belonged to wealthy passengers planning to proceed from California to the Hawaiian islands for an interlude of luaus and surfing while their less fortunate neighbors shivered in the Midwestern winter.

Whistler's eyes flicked back to Satin Blaine and caught her glancing involuntarily at a large suitcase. Clearly, it was of high quality but it was obviously well traveled. It bore stickers with scenes of Los Angeles, Honolulu, Singapore and Sydney.

Against one wall of the compartment, resting on a pair of wooden trestles, there lay a casket, its burnished bronze surface reflecting the dim electric lights in the ceiling. A light coating of frost gave its rounded lid the illusion of a graceful, snow-covered hillside. The very air near the casket was frigid.

'You boys are making things hard for me,' Satin Blaine hissed. 'As for Mr. Jenkins out there on the platform, if he'd just minded his business he would have been all right. That casket was sealed in Chicago and it shouldn't have been opened until we got to Los Angeles. Now I think I'll have to get off before then and leave my poor uncle to his own devices.'

The others waited for her to continue.

'What's our next stop, conductor?'

The railroad man went fishing in his vest pocket and came out with a huge old watch. He pressed a button and the engraved metal front of the timepiece popped open.

'Phoenix, Miss. We pass through around eleven tonight. Los Angeles in morning.'

'Okay, bub. Here's what we're going to do. I'm going to lock you in here. You — buster — the keys. That's right. Toss 'em gently.'

She caught the heavy collection of keys skillfully.

'I'm sure they'll wonder what happened to you, Mister Railroad Man, but that won't be my problem. And as for you two undertakers, just don't try anything clever and you'll stay alive.'

She edged toward the casket.

'All right, all three of you, step back. That's right. Undertakers first, so the railroad man is closest to me. I have a feeling you might try something, even risk getting shot at. You'd figure that I couldn't get both of you. Actually, I might. I'm a good shot. But you wouldn't risk an innocent man getting plugged. So you stay in front of the others, railroad man. Stay between me and them. If they try anything fancy, you get the first bullet, right in the belly. It's a lousy way to go, believe you me!'

What a nice little lady we've got here, don't you think? She looked so appealing up there in the club car, wouldn't any gentleman travelling alone on a stream-liner like the Desert Cannonball be happy to buy her a drink, just for the pleasure of her company? I guess the old saying is right. You know the one I mean. The one about appearances being deceiving.

Once the others had followed their instructions, Satin Blaine edged toward the casket. She managed to open her gold lamé purse with one hand and drop the keys into it, holding the gun on the others all the while. Then with her free hand she inserted long fingernails beneath the upper half of the divided coffin lid.

'Looks to me as if poor Mr. Jenkins opened this thing and then dropped the lid back in place when he ran away.'

It took a great effort by the slim Miss Blaine, but she managed to pry the lid open, then swing it back on its well-balanced hinges. As she did so a cloud of cold, white vapor rose from the casket and pooled around Satin Blaine's feet.

'All right. You — Mister Blackie there — I want you to open my valise.' She jerked her head toward the much-traveled suitcase, the one that was all but covered with the stickers from exotic ports of call.

'Dump my clothes out of there. I'll enjoy shopping for a new wardrobe anyhow.'

The face of the cadaver Satin Blaine had exposed was white, its eyebrows frosted like those of the late Oliver Jenkins. The body was dressed in a dark blue suit, white shirt and red necktie.

Satin Blaine glanced into the coffin. Still holding the .22 automatic on the others, she reached inside the suit jacket, then stepped back with a packet of large-denomination bills wrapped in a paper label. She tossed it across the car. It landed at the conductor's feet.

'Put that in the valise.'

As the railroad man complied she rummaged inside the casket, withdrawing packet after packet of currency and tossing them to the railroad man. As she worked she used them to knock white fuming cakes out of her way. White fuming cakes of dry ice, frozen squares of carbon dioxide, the coldest substance known to Man.

Suddenly she screamed.

The others jerked involuntarily, staring in amazement at the scene before them.

With a single spasmodic motion the cadaver had reached up and clutched the hand that had pulled bundle after bundle of money from the coffin.

'You can't do that — you're dead, dead!'

A horrifying moan rose from the casket.

Satin Blaine's arm was pulled toward the blue suit coat of the cadaver.

'I saw you die. I gave you the *conus purpurascens*, I put it in your shaving soap, I saw you collapse and die. You can't be alive. You can't be alive. You . . . '

The arm clutching her wrist drew her down, down, into the casket. As her face came close to that of the cadaver she screamed again and pulled the trigger of the pearl-handled automatic. It fired again and again, the bullets penetrating the body in the coffin.

Satin Blaine recoiled in a spasm of terror as her warm, lovely face made contact with the cold, white features of the cadaver. She flung herself backwards, her weapon flying from her hand and clattering against the opposite wall of the baggage car.

Traveler stepped forward and retrieved the weapon.

The woman collapsed against the bronze casket, one claw-like hand held in the unbreakable grip of the body in the casket. And it was now indeed a body, a dead body, a corpse. Ever since the poison of the Australian sea-cone had done its work, paralyzing Satin Blaine's Uncle Walter, some spark of life might have flickered faintly in the motionless body.

The .22-caliber rounds had extinguished that tiny, faint spark. And Satin Blaine had absorbed some of the toxin through her pale, delicate, lovely cheek.

Traveler steadied the trembling, fear-struck conductor.

'It's all right now, old man. There may even be a reward in it for you. You'd better message ahead to Phoenix and tell them to get in touch with the police in Chicago. The Farmers and Cattlemen's Bank loot is found.'

Oh, she was a clever one that *Satin Blaine*. She'd been to Australia, she'd managed to get ahold of the toxin of the Australian cone shell. These snails are among the deadliest creatures in the world. They appear harmless enough, their shells are even attractive-looking. But any tourist who picks one up — well, at least it's a painless death. Or so I've heard.

Myself, I wouldn't want to try it. Would you?

As for Uncle Walter — poor, dear Uncle Walter — do you think he really believed in vampires? I mean the human variety of vampires. Maybe he did. Maybe he was trying to become one. What was the famous line from Peter Pan? Oh yes. Do you believe in fairies? If you believe, clap your hands! *Well, dear friends — do you believe in vampires?*

As for that bat — there are plenty of bats in the desert. They're not really vampires. They live on insects. They're very useful little creatures, don't you know.

DOGWALKER

Farmer snapped his fingers and gestured and Bink, the big Rottie bitch, hopped out of the Olds Ciera and stood waiting for his next command. He snapped the chain-link leash onto her collar, patted her on the head and started into the park. She ambled along at his side, pausing here and there to sniff a tree-trunk, a clump of ivy or a fallen limb. She looked at Farmer as if she could talk him into throwing a stick for her, but he gave a tug at the leash and she assented, trotting now alongside his US Keds.

The park was narrow and winding, the equivalent of two or three city blocks in length, and blue maple and California scrub-oak limbs met overhead, making a shadowy tunnel that ran the length of the park, only a dappling of sunlight breaking through every few score yards.

He saw the old man with the basset heading toward him, the old man placing his feet gingerly, one ahead of the other, careful to avoid roots and rocks that might cause him to twist an ankle and tumble to the earth, bruising his aged flesh or, worse yet, fracturing a dry, aged leg or hipbone. The basset, overweight and clearly short on exercise, waddled and panted beside his master.

Farmer smiled and waved. 'Isn't it a glorious morning?'

The old man smiled back and mumbled something that Farmer couldn't make out, but it seemed vaguely agreeable. Farmer had seen the old man a few times before, in the park. Maybe it was the gray in Farmer's medium-length hair and in his mildly unkempt mustache that helped the old man feel comfortable with him.

Bink bent over the basset and snuffled. The basset made a soft sound and wagged its long tail.

Bink wiggled her own tiny, cropped tail and looked up at Farmer. He said, 'Come on, girl,' and to the old man, 'Have a great one,' and maneuvered the big Rottie around the old man and the fat basset and continued up the trail. He whistled a catchy tune he'd heard in an Alice Faye musical on AMC the night before. *You're a Sweetheart*. It stuck in his mind. *If there ever was one*. There was a kind of song, Farmer had never figured it out exactly, but they just did that to him. Just stuck in his mind. *If there ever was one, it's you*. Sometimes he thought he was in love with Alice Faye, even though she was born in 1915, the daughter of a cop, no less.

Traffic rolled past the park on either side, new Hondas and Acuras and Nissans, a Suzuki Samurai and a Mercedes, a family in a big Volvo wagon packed to the roof with camping and fishing gear, heading out on a wholesome family vacation.

Farmer heard voices approaching from behind him, and the crunching and rustling sounds of wheels rolling over dry twigs and brown leaves. He turned and saw a procession of boys and girls on bikes pedaling along the path. From the looks of them they averaged twelve years old. They were jabbering and screaming about their summer plans. Farmer stepped off the path, into a patch of lush green ivy. He pulled Bink with him and waved at the first of the bicyclists, a pretty girl with blonde hair streaming out from under her helmet.

The pretty girl waved back at Farmer as she wheeled past. She yelled, 'Thanks, Mister.' Farmer stood with his hand upraised, waving at the kids as they rolled along the path. Nice kids. Polite to an older man, as Farmer himself had been to the senior citizen walking his basset. Civil, their conduct was civil, as it ought to be.

Once the kids were past, Bink pulled him along the path impatiently. She leaped into the ivy, almost jerking Farmer off his feet. He yelled and caught his balance. 'Silly girl, you know you can't climb a tree. Leave the squirrels alone.' It had been a good winter, adequate rainfall for a change, not too cold. The spring vegetation had been lush and by summer the population of squirrels and birds in the parks had reached levels Farmer hadn't seen in years.

Halfway through the park a flight of cement steps led to the parallel street and the narrow sidewalk that marked the edge of the park. The houses that flanked the park varied in size and architecture. Those on the uphill side of the park were larger than those on the downhill side. There were Tudors and California Mission style homes and a few redwood or brown-shingle traditionals. No Victorians in this part of town; that style seemed not to fit in with the genteel suburban feel that the neighborhood managed to achieve despite its proximity to the university and the commercial areas that nourished the city's economy.

A classic little old lady was standing at the top of the cement steps. She clutched a leash, at the end of it a white toy poodle that squealed and tugged. The LOL grasped the metal handrail that slanted beside the steps. A look of panic swept across her papery features like the shadow of a fast-moving cloud sweeping across a leached-out, lifeless field.

Farmer found the encounter intriguing. He knew the poodle, even knew its name. He'd seen it walking sedately with a plainly dressed black woman on a number of occasions. But today, the person on the other end of the leash was this elderly female who gave off a distinct emanation of wealth.

Farmer laughed. 'There's nothing to be worried about.'

The LOL seemed to relax a little, but she still clung to the handrail and the poodle continued to pull. Farmer said, 'That's Dulcie, isn't it?'

The LOL nodded, seeming to relax a little more.

'This is Bink,' Farmer said. 'Bink and Dulcie are friends, see?' He let the Rottweiler approach the poodle. Dulcie squealed and rolled over. Bink nuzzled the poodle. The Rottie's squarish black-and-gold head was as big as the entire poodle.

The LOL relaxed some more. She reached a hand, tentatively, toward Bink, looking questioningly at Farmer. He said, 'It's okay, Bink loves people, don't you Binky girl?'

The Rottie wagged her stubby tail and massive hindquarters.

'We meet Dulcie almost every day,' Farmer said. 'But usually the other lady always walks her. I hope . . . ' He let the sentence trail away. The LOL would probably finish it for him. He was counting on that. He could see the hand on the iron rail, not the one holding the leash, was decorated with an expensive wedding ring and a matching engagement ring with a rock on it that set his mind to dancing.

'Oh, Claudie is my maid.'

'I'd never have known.'

'She's my friend, too.'

I'll just bet she is, Farmer thought.

'She's been with me ever so long. Years and years.'

Yes, but? There has to be a yes but, Farmer thought. Yes, but what?

'I couldn't get along without her. Especially since my husband . . . '

This time it was the LOL who let the sentence drift into silence. In that silence a motorcycle roared past, the driver gunning the engine as he climbed the hill.

'I understand,' Farmer said, even though he didn't. He had an idea, he had an inkling, and a gentle breeze stirred the scrub-oak leaves over the stairs letting a shaft of bright sunlight through to dance off the LOL's diamond ring. Yes, Farmer definitely had an idea. 'And Claudette — '

'No, just Claudie. You know, they have these funny names sometimes.'

'But she's still your friend.'

'Of course.'

'Claudie.'

'Oh, her grandmother, she told me, you know they live so long sometimes, but her grandmother, and of course I couldn't insist that she stay. She offered to get me someone while she's gone. Especially since my husband . . . '

'Of course, your husband.'

'But I told her, No, you go ahead, your family has to come first. I can manage. You come back as soon as you can. I'll take care of everything while you're away.'

The poodle sniffed at a pile of leaves, turned in a circle, and squatted. The LOL looked at Farmer.

'Well, I think Binky wants to get home for her breakfast.' Farmer extended his hand to the LOL. She looked confused for a moment, then transferred Dulcie's leash to the hand holding the railing and shook Farmer's hand with the other.

'A pleasure,' Farmer said. 'I hope Claudia's grandmother gets better soon, and I'll see you and Dulcie here, Mrs . . . '

The LOL's hand was like a dry, empty husk in Farmer's. He had to be careful not to crush it. Not to crush it. 'Mrs . . . ' he said again.

'Clyde,' she furnished, even though he'd had to clue her twice to get the answer. 'And Claudie, not Claudia.'

Farmer shook his head self-deprecatingly. 'I'm terrible about names. Terrible. Mine is Farmer. You know, sometimes I think I'm going to forget my own name. But I always remember pets. I'd never forget Bink. Or Dulcie. Well, then . . . '

He let Bink lead him up the path, turned back for an instant and saw Mrs. Clyde and Dulcie heading in the opposite direction, the LOL walking steadily in sensible shoes and a dress. You never saw women in dresses in the park, but Mrs. Clyde was an exception.

Bink and Farmer reached the top of the park, headed out and across the street, then walked back to where he'd left the Olds Ciera. He unlocked the passenger-side door and said, 'Okay, Bink old girl, let's go home.' The Rottie jumped in the car and settled down on the faded upholstery. Farmer thought, I ought to get her a mat or something before she wears right through that seat. He walked around the car and opened the driver's-side door and climbed in. On the way home he listened to an oldies station. After a commercial the disk jockey put on a cover version of *You Turned the Tables on Me*, another Alice Faye standard, by some present day vocalist. She was plenty good, but she was no Alice Faye.

At home he put out Bink's breakfast and set to work with a telephone book and a city map. There were a dozen Clydes listed. Farmer searched for their addresses on the city map. He managed to eliminate eight that way. They just didn't live any-where near the park, and he knew that Mrs. Clyde — *his* Mrs. Clyde — wouldn't have come from another neighborhood just to walk Dulcie in the park.

Of the four remaining Clydes, two were

listed as *Mr. and Mrs.* Farmer eliminated them. The elimination tourney was down to the finals. One of the two remaining Clydes was listed as *P. Clyde, DDS*. The other was simply, *R. Clyde*, and an address that Farmer knew was just a stone's throw from the park even without checking the map. Many women listed their telephone numbers with only first initials. Nice, androgynous initials. They discouraged obscene phone calls, or they had, maybe, until the obscene phone callers had caught on to the trick.

Farmer knew that *R. Clyde, 55 Ferndale*, was his Mrs. Clyde. R. Was she Roberta? Rachel? Rona, Rhonda, Rolanda?

Close attention to detail, that was the key to success in any business, including Farmer's. He chose his targets with care, did not strike too often, did not return to a neighborhood where he had previously worked. He had never been arrested, never been in serious trouble, earned a good living for himself, had money in the bank and conservative investments in his portfolio and lived a quiet, respectable life in his comfortable home with his faithful four-legged companion.

Farmer went into the bathroom and scrubbed the gray out of his hair and mustache, and combed his hair carefully and brushed his mustache into neat order. He smiled ruefully at his reflection. Mother Nature was doing her work. It wouldn't be long, at this rate, before he had to *cover* the gray instead of adding it, to change his appearance.

He let Bink out in the back yard to do her stuff, then they spent half an hour on their drills. Bink was good at the drills, she was one smart bitch, and Farmer ought to know. He loved Bink. Love, that was part of the secret of his success.

Actually she was Bink III. He'd raised the first Bink from a puppy, had built his career with her help, and had cried hot, salty tears when he'd had her put down. She was getting old and her hips were starting to go. These big, heavy dogs just didn't have the longevity of smaller, lighter breeds.

And then there had been Bink II. Rottweiler pups were expensive, but Farmer wouldn't settle for less than the best. And in due course Bink II had gone the way of Bink I, and Farmer had cried again, and taken some time off, and then bought Bink III and started training her. She was a great bitch, maybe the best of the three. By the time she was ready to retire, if things went well, he might be ready to do the same.

It was quite a thought.

He had a class at the community college that night, and he took Bink with him and made her stay in the Ciera while he sat through the lecture. He never used his real name when he enrolled in courses, and between such simple precautions, and moving on every so often, he figured he'd never get his degree. But what the heck, the classes were interesting and they filled the empty evenings. And once in a while he met some lonely divorcee or plain-featured middle-aged woman, and had a fling. Nobody ever got hurt, more empty evenings got filled, and when he moved on he left pleasant memories behind to warm those lonely hearts on cold, lonely evenings.

The next day, after he'd added the gray

to his hair and mustache, he let Bink out as usual. They ran through a training session, then he brought her back through the house and out the front door. They jumped into the Ciera and drove back to the park. Farmer parked the Ciera on Wilton, just off Ferndale a couple of blocks from number 55.

He walked Bink along Wilton, then turned onto Ferndale, casing the houses. He kept an eye out for pedestrians or nosy neighbors. Ferndale was a quiet street. There was nothing pretentious about it. This wasn't a section for the super-wealthy. There were few if any of them in this town. But the people who lived on Ferndale were upper middle class. Very upper. They tended to have good jewelry and often serious cash in their houses. Certainly Mrs. R. Clyde had jewelry. Nice and compact and portable and convertible jewelry. And Claudie was out of town because of her grandmother. And since Mrs. Clyde's husband . . .

Farmer smiled to himself.

Number 55 Ferndale was a Tudor, down to the white stucco and half-timbers and the kitschy diamond-pane windows. A winding driveway led to an attached double garage. A row of firs lined the driveway, blocking part of the house's well-tended lawn from the street.

Perfect.

Perfect.

He strolled around the neighborhood waiting for Mrs. Clyde to emerge from her house with Dulcie. Or — huh, maybe he'd blown the timing and the LOL was already out walking her poodle. Well, that was okay too. He just wanted to meet them again, wanted Mrs. Clyde to see him and Bink once more, preferably nearer her house than the park. Just to get her accustomed to the idea.

Just as he was thinking of giving up, of putting the whole project off 'til tomorrow, he heard a soft voice. 'Mister — was it Mister — '

He turned around, smiling. 'Farmer,' he said. 'And you're Missus, uh — I'm so bad with names.'

She smiled back at him. 'Mrs. Clyde.' Dulcie yapped.

'Maybe I'm just getting old,' he said.

She shook her head. 'Oh, no. You're a young man, Mr. Farmer.'

He gave her his grateful look. 'At least I remember Dulcie's name. I never forget pets.'

Mrs. Clyde said, 'Do you live near here, Mr. Farmer?'

'Fairly. It's just that Bink loves the little park so, and I enjoy looking at the lovely houses. Is one of them yours?' As if he didn't know damned well which was hers.

'Oh, the Tudor, you see.' She gestured. 'My husband and I built that house. Forty-three years ago. Forty-three years.' She took a breath. 'But since he — I just don't know if I — '

Farmer assumed his sympathetic expression and nodded and mumbled.

Dulcie and Bink were sniffing each other. Mrs. Clyde said, 'You know, they say that certain breeds of dogs are so fierce. Dobermans and pit bulls and Rottweilers.'

Farmer shook his head. 'Not if you love them. Not if you raise them to be gentle and to know love and not violence. Just look at those two.' He laughed.

Mrs. Clyde pulled back a sleeve of her

expensive dress. The sky was clear again today, and the sun glinted on a diamond-studded wristwatch. Farmer admired it silently. Mrs. Clyde looked a little concerned.

Farmer said, 'Well, we shouldn't really keep you and Dulcie any longer. It's just such a pleasure — ' He reached down and scratched the poodle behind its ears. Its coat was as curly as a lamb's.

Mrs. Clyde said, 'It was so nice,' and tugged at Dulcie's leash, and headed back to number 55.

That night he got ready to move. He packed his few belongings: half a dozen favorite books, a few CDs (a couple of Sinatra compilations, Mary Martin's *Songs from Rodgers and Hammerstein's The Sound of Music*, and of course *Alice Faye's Greatest Hits*), and his little cable-ready TV. And of course Bink's spare water dish, dinner dish, her favorite toys, and her spare leash and collar.

It might be nice, someday, to own a house instead of always having to rent. But when your business kept you moving around the country, that just wasn't practical. He only had to hit once every few years, once every time he moved. He'd lived in Vermont, in Oklahoma, in New Jersey, in Florida, and now in northern California.

And of course he knew where he was headed next. He believed in careful planning. He was headed up north again, but not to Oregon. He had his eye on Idaho. Boise, Idaho.

He always hit the same way when he hit, when he and Bink hit. But each time out brought enough to last for years, and who was going to remember a hit five years ago and two or three thousand miles away? Farmer remembered. He remembered the little Sheltie in Montpelier and the miniature schnauzer in Enid and the unusual, wirehaired dachshund in that little town near Trenton. They bothered him, they really did, every one of them. But business was business. It was a safe way to work, and Farmer liked to be safe.

He got a good night's sleep. Bink always seemed to sense a big day coming up, and she climbed onto Farmer's bed when she thought he was asleep and snuggled against his legs and went to sleep, too. Farmer had a funny dream that night. He was in an old movie, wearing a scratchy woolen suit and a stiff-collared shirt, and Alice Faye was there in a low-cut Naughty Nineties gown and with an ostrich feather in her hair, and they were doing a song-and-dance act to the tune of *You Say the Sweetest Things Baby*. He woke up and the woolen blanket was itching under his chin. He rubbed his eyes, reached down and rubbed Bink's muscular flank and climbed out of bed.

An hour later he parked the Ciera a couple of blocks from Mrs. Clyde's house and got out of the car. He was in his gray-hair-and-mustache persona. He snapped the leash on Bink's collar, took a small plastic bottle out of the Ciera's trunk, and walked the Rottie toward Mrs. Clyde's house. Farmer looked around cautiously, led Bink into the cover of the firs and knelt beside her. He pulled a large, heavy-gauge rubber band from his pocket and worked it up over Bink's right front leg, all the way to the shoulder. He opened the plastic bottle and poured its contents over

Bink's right front shoulder. He tossed the empty bottle into the fir trees. He straightened up, grasped Bink's leash in his hand and started running toward the front door of number 55.

He wasn't in great shape, actually, and he managed to look disheveled by the time they reached the front door. He was panting a little, maybe a little more than he needed to. Bink had tried to run with him, but the heavy rubber band around her shoulder was uncomfortable and she wound up with a limping, rolling gate.

Farmer pounded on the door, gasping and calling softly, as if he didn't have the breath to raise his voice, to be let in. Bink raised her dripping and rubber-banded leg and scratched at the door.

After a few seconds that seemed like a year, the door swung back a couple of inches. Mrs. Clyde looked out, her pale blue eyes wide and her china-white skin looking more delicate than ever. Somewhere out of sight, the toy poodle Dulcie was yapping.

Farmer gasped, 'That hoodlum! He hit poor Binky and he never even stopped.

He could have stopped. He could have taken us to the vet's.'

The rubber band must have made Bink's shoulder sore because she whined and bit at it. Perfect. *Perfect.*

'Can you — she's bleeding.' Some of the phony blood from the plastic bottle must have splashed on Farmer's face. He hadn't even thought of that, but it was even better that way.

Mrs. Clyde said, 'Mr. Farmer — '

'Please — Binky.'

'Of course. Come — '

She stepped away from the door. Farmer pushed it wide open. He took a couple of wobbly steps inside, Bink leaning against his thigh. Mrs. Clyde said, 'I'll telephone. They'll send somebody.'

Farmer sank to his knees. He put his arms around Bink and worked the heavy rubber band loose. More of the phony blood got on his face and hands. Mrs. Clyde had picked up the telephone. Little Dulcie had run into the room and was staring at Bink.

The room had a high, cathedral ceiling with dark wooden beams. The walls carried out the kitschy Tudor theme. The floor was of huge flagstones with expensive-looking area rugs and an antique-looking refectory table.

Dulcie had run up to Bink. The big Rottie leaned over the poodle, baring her teeth. The poodle rolled on her back, squealing.

Farmer surveyed the room one last time, to make sure that everything was right. It was. 'Now, Binky, get 'er!'

Mrs. Clyde and Dulcie screamed simultaneously as Bink sank her teeth into the poodle's guts. She picked up the poodle, gave it one furious shake and flung it across the room. The poodle's screaming stopped as it smacked against the refectory table and tumbled onto a rug. Mrs. Clyde's screaming got louder.

Farmer pointed at the LOL and grunted, 'Now, Binky, get 'er!'

The Rottweiler sprang at the old woman.

Farmer heard a whining sound and looked around. From a back hallway, an electric wheelchair rolled steadily into the room. The man in it was ancient, wizened. A lap-robe covered him from the waist down. Farmer hadn't seen anything like that since some Raymond Chandler flick on TV.

The old man.

Mrs. Clyde had said, 'Since my husband . . . ' And again, 'Since my husband . . . ' Farmer had thought she meant, since her husband had died, and was too bereft to speak the words. But she must have meant, since her husband became crippled.

But only from the waist down.

From the waist up he looked okay. Old and weak, but okay. And too far away from Farmer or from Bink for either of them to keep him from firing the double-barreled shotgun that he was pointing in front of him.

Still, Farmer pointed at the old man and ordered, 'Now, Binky, get 'im!'

The Rottweiler abandoned what was left of Mrs. Clyde and charged across the room. Farmer saw the flash of the shotgun, then heard its explosion, then felt the impact of a full load of pellets smash into his chest and hurl him back through the still-open front door. He looked straight up at the brilliant afternoon sky. He heard the shotgun roar a second time but he didn't know whether Mr. Clyde had hit Binky or missed her.

THE END